Praise for *Mu*

"A razor-sharp delight! What a t̶r̶e̶a̶t̶ i̶t̶ i̶s̶ t̶o̶ h̶a̶v̶e̶ a̶ w̶o̶n̶d̶e̶r̶f̶u̶l̶ a̶n̶d̶ w̶i̶t̶t̶y̶ mash-up of a murder mystery and onstage/offstage intrigue. I look forward to seeing where the intrepid Asher Kaufman goes next!"

— Tom Ford, director/actor, Sweeney Todd portrayer at the Great Lakes Theater and the Lake Tahoe Shakespeare Festival

"By turning a dark musical into a delightful whodunit, Abelman one-ups Stephen Sondheim and Agatha Christie. I didn't want it to end."

— Fred Sternfeld, Broadway producer, Stage Directors and Choreographers Society member

"*All the World's a Stage Fright's* Asher Kaufman is back on stage and Abelman ramps up the humor and the stakes. The writing is sharp and clever. The characters are well-drawn. And the whodunit carries you right to the end. You'll have a ball."

— Rich Leder, novelist/screenwriter and author of the *Kate McCall Crime Caper* series

"This novella is a wonderful, intelligent, and delightful escape. I loved everything about it!"

—Terri Kent, producing artistic director, Porthouse Theatre

"Abelman's cut-above (yes, pun intended) novella is an unapologetic homage to theater. And it is just damn fun!"

— Marc Moritz, actor and original Broadway cast member of the Sondheim/Prince musical *Merrily We Roll Along*

"A total page turner! *Murder, Center Stage* is a must-read novella filled with suspense, humor, and more than a little cheekiness."

— Donald Carrier, actor and director of the Case Western Reserve University/Cleveland Play House MFA Acting Program

"Bob Abelman's tale of theatrical mayhem with a bloody dose of Stephen Sondheim's *Sweeney Todd* will keep readers guessing about motives and machinations. The colorful characters keep the story moving. I suspect theater fans will give *Murder, Center Stage* a standing ovation.

— Rick Pender, theater critic at Cincinnati *CityBeat* and author of *The Stephen Sondheim Encyclopedia*

ALSO BY BOB ABELMAN
All the World's a Stage Fright

Murder, Center Stage

Misadventures of a Clandestine Critic

— A NOVELLA —

Bob Abelman

Published in partnership with
Cleveland Jewish News

Gray & Company, Publishers
Cleveland

Gray & Company, Publishers
www.grayco.com

ISBN 978-1-59851-121-5
Printed in the United States of America

Contents

Murder,
Center Stage

Chapter 1

All of Us Deserve to Die

THE ROUGH DRAFT first paragraph of Gwen's review of the musical *Sweeney Todd: The Demon Barber of Fleet Street* was typed out on her computer just before she left her near west side efficiency apartment for downtown Cleveland's Hedley Theatre. It read:

> All of us deserve to die. So sings the homicidal [or deranged, perhaps unhinged] title character in *Sweeney Todd*, which reinforces the pitch-black theme that drives this remarkably angry, bleak, and brilliant musical. Set in grimy [or grungy or decaying] 19th century London, we find the barber avenging his wrongful imprisonment and the senseless destruction of his fledgling family by whittling away at his clueless clientele and turning the fruits of his labor into meat pies to be sold in the shop below.

The paragraph was to be revised and the review fleshed out with astute observations, carefully honed opinions, and clever writing upon her return from the sold-out opening night show. It would then be posted in time for tomorrow morning's deadline and published in the next issue of the *Chronicle*. Instead, it was recovered from Gwen's laptop by the police.

The notepad she used while watching the North Coast

Theater production was no doubt filled with insightful reflections about this evening's performance—the acting choices, the rendering of Sweeney's decrepit Fleet Street dwelling, and the goth-inspired costuming. Very little was legible because of the blood.

Chapter 2

Doing a Plimpton

G WEN HAD BEEN warned about the hazards of the job.
An intense, accomplished, and overachieving sopho-
more at a local Jesuit college, she easily made the short list
for the intern position at the newspaper that had hired me
as its theater critic. As we toured the artificially bright and
authentically busy newsroom on the way to an interview with
Mark, the managing assistant editor of the *Chronicle* and my
boss—me completely fabricating a running, rambling narra-
tive about how things operate around here and Gwen dili-
gently writing down everything—I clued her in on the perils
that awaited her in a life dedicated to arts journalism.

"It's not all fame, fun, and fortune," I told her. "Taking
notes with a pen in a small spiral notebook in a darkened
theater is a high-risk enterprise not for the faint of heart. I'm
a seasoned professional, yet most of my note-taking ends up
on the right thigh of my pants. I've taken to wearing light tan
khakis to the theater to best facilitate the late-night transcrip-
tions." She jotted this down, missing the pad she held and
leaving a blue trail of words on the palm of her hand. Bonus
points for a working sense of humor.

"There's also the loss of a normal social life when all your
Friday and Saturday nights are spent at a theater." Her blank
expression and lack of response suggested that "normal" for

her meant "nonexistent," which was an ideal lifestyle choice for a highly overworked intern.

"Overnight deadlines can be quite stressful," I added, although I knew from having read her lengthy resume and impressive letters of recommendation that tight turnaround was more of an enticement than a deterrent for a chronic go-getter like her.

"And there's the very real likelihood of making enemies within the arts community when the job requires a very public critique of their work, which influences their professional reputations and impacts their livelihoods." When she said that this was the "price a critic pays for being a referee of the muses," we skipped the interview and I welcomed her to the paper.

Gwen and I shook on it, and some of the blue ink from her sweaty palm transferred to mine.

"Well, I suppose that's better than spitting on our hands to seal the deal," I said.

"I guess we're pen pals," she countered.

Since then, over the past six months, Gwen has served as a reliable proofreader, all-purpose gofer, and occasional beat reporter.

I have been with the *Chronicle* for about twenty years, reviewing the dozens of regional playhouses, classic repertory companies, and national tours that make up the thriving Cleveland theater scene. But prior to my life as a theater critic, I had been a professional actor. I quickly realized that the name Asher Kaufman would be better placed in the byline of a show's review than in the *dramatis personae* of its playbill. I got work, but almost always in small supporting roles in plays penned by Schwartzes, Bernsteins, and Simons. I once asked a casting agent what it would take for someone who looked like me—short, solid, and alluringly Ashkenazi—to land a romantic lead in something other than a play chronicling the Jewish diaspora or taking place during the Holocaust. She said, "the unexpected comeback of radio drama."

And so I left the stage, just not the theater.

But I recently dusted off my acting skills and landed a small role in North Coast Theater's production of Shakespeare's comedy *As You Like It* so that I could write about the experience. The professional theater company is a partnership organization that shares production costs and performances with another theater, so *As You Like It* was rehearsed and opened in Cleveland before moving to the Taos Shakespeare Festival in New Mexico for an additional three-week run.

The idea that I write a series of articles about what takes place on the other side of the proscenium arch came from my boss, Mark. The man is straight out of central casting from the classic 1928 stage comedy *The Front Page,* where characters are fast-talking, hard-boiled, big-city newshounds who somehow come across as appealing and approachable. Like them, he wears suspenders, as if the news cycle was so unrelenting that there was no time to strap on a belt. There's no explanation for his bow tie.

He called our clandestine operation "doing a Plimpton," noting that it was named after the American journalist who, in 1963, attended the preseason training camp of the Detroit Lions of the National Football League under the pretense of being a backup quarterback. Plimpton also wrote about sparring boxing champion Archie Moore, who, at the time, had a record of 171-22-9, earned largely by having great defense and a strong chin. Neither was required when he met the journalist in the ring, who was an intellectual heavyweight but pugilistic lightweight. Plimpton, a glutton for punishment, also wrote about absorbing slap shots as an ice hockey goalie with the Boston Bruins.

Treading the boards seemed so much saner and safer, so I thought I'd give it a go.

The *As You Like It* experience was, in a word, terrifying. I found myself struggling to memorize Elizabethan prose, wrestling with iambic pentameter, and failing to keep pace with the very same classically trained, passive-aggressive North Coast Theater company members whom I had brutally panned in the past. Prior to this, the only Shakespeare I've ever performed professionally was *The Taming of the Shrew*, but only after Cole Porter had transformed it into the lovable musical *Kiss Me, Kate.*

Mark was ecstatic about the interest my painful and very public attempt at experiential journalism sparked among the paper's readers and advertisers. And he was delighted to have my awkward opening night attempt at Shakespeare-speak reviewed by Gwen, who was starting to find her voice as a journalist at my expense.

He was still supportive when the company offered to cast me in its next production, Stephen Sondheim's challenging musical *Sweeney Todd*. This was a North Coast Theater decision clearly based on the publicity I offer a production by writing about it and not necessarily what I bring to the stage as a performer in an ensemble role. Famous theater practitioner Michael Chekhov, a nephew of playwright Anton Chekhov and a student of performance guru Konstantin Stanislavski, once said that "an actor has to burn inside with an outer ease" to win over an audience. These days, I tend to embrace the advice of the Hippocratic oath in my acting: "First, do no harm."

Sweeney Todd's dense and difficult lyrics, demanding vocal range, and enigmatic melodies meant more engaging backstage stories chronicling my terror, and playing a small role would suffice for our purposes. After all, Plimpton got only five snaps during his short time as a backup quarterback for the Lions, stood for only five minutes in the crease for the Bruins, and sparred only three rounds with Archie Moore.

Of course, the driven and ever-opportunistic Gwen—who has a 4.1 GPA at her Jesuit college, is co-editor of her campus newspaper, and serves as captain of her school's épée fencing and debate clubs—once again jumped at the chance to get a running byline in the paper during my absence for *Sweeney's* rehearsals and run in Taos, and she was more than happy to review the show during opening night when it returned to Cleveland a few weeks later.

I often joked that, if there were such a thing as competitive prayer at her school, Gwen would be its record holder. She often joked that, if I ever got hit by a meteor from space or, less probably, if *The New York Times* came a-calling for my services, she would be happy to make my column her own.

Chapter 3

Shave and a Haircut, Two Bits

THE OPENING NIGHT production of *Sweeney Todd* has been halted and I've been sitting in the sixth row of the Hedley Theatre for about an hour now. After the gruesome murder that had taken place mid-production in front of a standing-room-only crowd, management ordered everyone in the audience to quickly move into the lobby and everyone on stage and backstage to take a seat in the house until the Cleveland police arrived.

To clear my head, pass the time, and help keep my eyes from gravitating toward the bloody body hastily covered with a linen sheet at center stage, I busy myself by looking at all the things I've taken for granted about the theater during my many visits as a critic. I trace the mosaic pattern deeply woven into the burgundy carpeting. I notice the Italian Renaissance architecture infused with the bold contemporary sensibilities introduced during the recent renovation. I tilt my head back and take in the ornamental rosettes, acanthus leaves, and assorted curlicues that decorate the crown molding that surrounds the house ceiling and start counting the crystals in the antique chandeliers dangling from the ceiling.

While doing so, I find myself mindlessly humming the tune "Johanna" from *Sweeney Todd,* which is an odd subconscious choice. The song occurs early in the second act of the musical, once Sweeney's makeshift salon above Mrs. Lovett's meat pie shop has become his personal slaughterhouse. As he sings, audiences witness the sociopathic barber executing one innocent customer after another in anticipation of slaying the ones who had preyed on his trust and his young family years ago.

Unlike the largely confessional and anguished songs that come before and after, "Johanna" is beautifully melodic. It serves as a startling and morbid juxtaposition to the senseless, emotionless, repetitive killing taking place on stage. To make sure audiences know that the melodic nature of the song is meant to be deeply sardonic—for nothing will end well for any of the characters in this macabre musical—the genius Sondheim added a final dissonant chord that is slightly off-key, held just a little too long, and falls oddly on the ear.

This song must be on my mind because the orchestra never made it to that dissonant chord during this evening's performance. It stopped playing upon the onstage slaughter of North Coast Theater's producing artistic director, Andrew Ganz.

Andrew had been somehow substituted for the young actor who was supposed to be sitting in Sweeney's barber chair at the start of the song. The prop straight-blade razor used by the actor playing Sweeney had been swapped out for a real one and, with it, Andrew was publicly executed in front of shocked friends, sickened board members, and five hundred avid theatergoers and season subscribers.

In the script, the actor playing Sweeney mimics the execution of a local Londoner with a prop razor that squirts stage blood when pressure is applied to the blade with the middle finger. Just before the second in a series of customers pops into the barbershop for similar treatment, the faux-blood-dowsed actor in the barber chair is to slide off and fall through a trap door in the floor by his feet. A chute takes him down through the hidden interior of the two-story set piece. It deposits him through a pair of swinging doors onto the stage, which serves as the basement where the meat pies are made, and—by way of momentum and a well-rehearsed pratfall designed by a professional stage fight choreographer—into a small pile of life-like mannequins with similarly bloodied throats that awaits him in the dark shadows.

But after Andrew's too-long, too-limp, near-dead body made the precarious journey down the chute, it flopped gracelessly through the swinging doors, tumbled past the pile of mannequins, ran out of momentum, and landed awkwardly in a tangled mass at the edge of the darkened stage and right in front of Gwen. She and her fellow patrons in the first two rows—many of them critics from other publications—were sprayed with beads of ruby-red liquid, courtesy of the artistic director's freshly severed and spectacularly squirting jugular.

As a career thespian turned affable artistic director, everything the handsome middle-aged Andrew did in life was theatrical. Even his full head of wavy, insolent, light brown hair managed to find its way into one eye or the other so it could be affectedly swept away with a flick of his left hand. He didn't just enter a room; he ENTERED a room, and his tragic, hideous demise on stage was certainly no less ostentatious. While Sondheim would have been horrified by Andrew's death, he would not have been disappointed by how dramatically it unfolded.

Drenched in what she assumed was washable stage blood, Gwen registered a mental note about the production's need for a designated splash zone and continued watching the show. After a minute or two, when the fluid that coated the modest but attractive ecru dress she had bought for opening night and matted down her mousy brown hair that took way too long to tame started to thicken, she realized that the blood was the real deal. She realized, too, that the grotesque figure that was gurgling its final breath while bleeding out was the real deal as well. And so she screamed. She screamed loud and she screamed long.

When others in the audience realized that the scream was coming from the seats and not the stage—the acoustics in the newly renovated Hedley Theatre are remarkable—they quickly snapped out of the trance that vicarious experience in the dark can induce. Jarred from the violent fantasy of the play and into an identically graphic reality, they screamed as well.

At the moment of Andrew's near-beheading, I was standing on a stage left platform that accesses the second-story barbershop, just out of view of the audience. As I've done every night leading up to this performance, I was nervously envisioning my entrance and counting the beats in the song "Johanna" that led to my musical cue to be Sweeney's second customer.

Sweeney singing "And if I never hear your voice, my turtle-dove, my dear" is when I come into view from stage left, nod at Sweeney as I head for the now-unoccupied barber chair, and remove my bowler hat with my upstage hand.

"I still have reason to rejoice the way ahead is clear, Johanna" is when I take a seat in the chair and Sweeney drapes me in a white barber's cape that covers everything but my shoes. I tilt my head back slightly so he can tuck the cape in around the high collar of my costume.

"And in that darkness when I'm blind with what I can't forget" is when I tilt my head back even farther as my face and throat are quickly lathered for the close shave to come.

"It's always morning in my mind, my little lamb, my pet, Jo-han-na" is when the prop razor navigates my throat from left ear to right ear, leaving a crimson trail of stage blood—a thick concoction made of corn syrup, red food color, cocoa powder and cornstarch mixed with distilled water. Sweeney then pulls the lever that opens the trap door while singing: "You stay, Johanna, the way I dreamed you are. Oh look, Johanna, a star." The chair tilts up and down I slide.

This is simple stage blocking, really. But a Sondheim musical requires the kind of precision and intensity that has me second-guessing my preparation and stirs a deep-rooted fear of failure that so many actors possess, but which I have in spades. My insecurity is so severe that I occasionally have those crazy late-night dreams about being naked in a public place, of being watched and judged by strangers while standing exposed and defenseless. Only I'm in a pair of light tan khakis.

By the time the stage manager sitting in the control booth on the mezzanine level at the back of the house noticed Andrew's awkward tumble across the stage on her black-and-white monitor, heard the screaming, and called "halt" over the theater's sound system—as cast members froze, the orchestra stopped playing, the house lights came up, and Gwen continued to scream—Sweeney's sharp blade was at the crook of my neck and nicking the thin skin that covered the carotid artery just below the surface. Following the source of the screaming, my eyes glanced down at the bloody stage and the cause of the commotion, and I immediately did the math.

Grabbing the razor-bearing arm of the actor playing Sweeney—a talented and unlikable Tony nominee brought in from New York City to play the show's title role—I stood, pivoted, drove my shoulder hard into his chest just as he was singing "Jo-han-na," and plowed him into the ground. The final syllable, all the air in his lungs, and a modicum of spittle were expelled upon impact.

There was a lot going on inside my head as I lay on top of the startled, gasping performer, all of it random, irrational, and fleeting. I tried to recall the Broadway play for which this actor was nominated. I worried that tackling Sweeney would get me in deep trouble with the actors' union. And, as Sweeney's terrified, confused eyes met mine, I wondered about Gwen's headline in tomorrow morning's review in the *Chronicle*.

Chapter 4

A Broadway Dream Deferred

F ROM THE EDITOR: This is the first in a series of behind-the-scenes articles by critic Asher Kaufman about his adventures in North Coast Theater's production of *Sweeney Todd*. The show is currently in rehearsal in Taos, New Mexico, and opens in Cleveland in five weeks.

The most popular myth about Broadway is the one perpetuated by the 1933 musical *42nd Street*, in which an unknown chorus girl goes on in place of the leading lady and becomes a star.

Few actors would confess to being naive enough to believe this fantasy. But none would deny that the prospect of instantaneous success on the New York stage had crossed their minds and fueled their enterprise while taking endless voice and dance lessons as a child, during competitive auditions for the high school drama club, and while rigorously training at a performing arts conservatory. It resurfaces during every professional production that is not taking place on Broadway.

Sure, they've seen the statistics. Hell, they're living them.

Only thirty-eight percent of the 50,000 professional actors who make up the membership of the Actors' Equity

Association work at any given time. And they typically work an average of only seventeen weeks a year, earning $15,000 or less, and do so on stages far from the glamour of the New York City theater scene.

Even if they get cast in a Broadway-bound show, most shows fail in tryouts on regional theater stages before they even arrive in New York City, and eighty percent of shows that open on Broadway close quickly and lose money. For every *Wicked*, which earned over $1 billion in box office sales from its more than 6,800 performances at the Gershwin Theatre, there are plenty of *Nerds*, a musical about the rivalry between Steve Jobs and Bill Gates, which ironically ran out of money and abruptly canceled its Broadway debut just weeks before it was scheduled to begin performances.

But actors have also heard the success stories of colleagues who made it to the theater district that extends from West 40th to West 54th Streets, between 6th and 8th Avenues. And, of course, they've memorized the original Broadway cast soundtrack to *42nd Street*, which reinforces the fantasy.

Clearly, the road to The Great White Way is full of speed bumps, unexpected detours, and dead ends. So what happens to a Broadway dream deferred? Does it, in the words of poet Langston Hughes, "dry up like a raisin in the sun?"

Meet Chris O'Connell, who is playing the romantic lead, Anthony, in our production of *Sweeney Todd*. "Two years ago, I graduated from the University of Cincinnati College-Conservatory of Music and moved right away to my brother's couch in NYC to start auditioning. I was waking up at 4 a.m. to be the first one in line at every Broadway opportunity."

After months of auditioning, exercising, and dance and vocal training classes, Chris came across a Disney Cruise Line audition call and couldn't pass up the prospect of work. Two days later, he went in for callbacks and, two days after that, he got the gig. On board, he performed twice a night in one of four rotating shows—a musical revue featuring characters from Disney films, a show consisting of big production numbers from Disney Broadway musicals, a more intimate cabaret show, and a staged production of *Toy Story*.

Chris is thankful for the intense eight-month cruise experience and was happy to sign up for eight months more when asked, but, while at sea, he felt that every port of call took him further away from Broadway. When he returned to the city, he discovered that—even at twenty-three years of age—he was now a year-and-a-half older and less familiar to casting agents than all the young bloods showing up for auditions with the same good looks, the same skills, and a year-and-a-half's worth of New York theater experience. He has since settled into a career as an itinerant actor, working as a jobber with regional companies throughout the country, like North Coast Theater.

"My life in the American theater has not been defined by whether or not I get to Broadway," says Chris. "It is the inner drive and need and passion to do what it is I do." But when asked what he would do if the opportunity to perform in a Broadway theater ever came his way, his response was, "I'd jump at it in a second. And not let anything or anyone get in my way."

Meet Erin Andrews, who plays Johanna—the romantic lead opposite Chris' Anthony—in *Sweeney Todd*. Her Broadway dream was inclusive enough to embrace performing in a national tour of a Broadway show. A tour means a regular gig for a guaranteed time, which is more than a Broadway engagement can promise. And an Equity tour means a big production budget, a big paycheck, and attractive travel accommodations that include more planes than buses. Touring in what was a bona fide Broadway hit also fills theater seats, which means playing to big houses.

Prior to joining the North Coast Theater company, Erin was booked on a non-Equity tour of *Jersey Boys*. That meant fewer creature comforts on the road—months of bus travel only, motels rather than hotels, and living out of a suitcase in a different city every day or two, rather than every few weeks. The production itself had significantly fewer bells and whistles than the Equity tour, and the performance schedule either hit the smaller cities that the Equity tour dismissed or doubled back on larger cities, trying to find an audience among those who somehow missed the Equity show the first few times around. She performed in Cleveland and found that the audiences were small after Equity touring companies had already passed through three times over the past five years.

"Tours can be grueling, lonely, and tedious," admits Erin, "but at least you are doing what you love. Have always loved. But, sure, I would kill to be on Broadway."

For performers like Chris, Erin, and so many others, the road to Broadway can only be seen in the rearview mirror as other opportunities to be an artist and earn a living doing so avail themselves. But there is always the hope of someday making it on the New York stage. After all, they still listen to the original Broadway cast soundtrack to *42nd Street* and, as the message in the tempered glass of the rearview mirror declares—no, promises—objects may be closer than they appear.

Chapter 5

Slaying 'em in the Aisles

A SMALL BRIGADE OF ushers in red blazers, most of them in
their eighties and half the size of their former selves, have
been instructed by the house manager to keep the hundreds of
opening night attendees from leaving the theater lobby until
the police arrive. Our stage is now an official crime scene.

By the time the police do arrive, the complaints are many
and the tension is high. And that's coming from the ushers.
Audience members—most in shock, some weeping, and a few
terribly put out by the inconvenience of having their Friday
evening ruined—are growing impatient and more than eager
to make their exit. I can hear from where I sit in the house the
collective muttering of the mob in the lobby and the occasional rising and falling cries of ancient ushers as they are
swallowed up by the sea of irate theatergoers, only to be lifted
above the throng for a moment and—gasping for breath with
arms flailing as they reach the crest—are swallowed again.

The still-costumed cast in stage makeup and members of
the twelve-piece orchestra have been sequestered in the plush,
burgundy dress circle seating I share. So have the show's
music director/conductor and the director who, just a short
while ago, was seated next to his wife and a vibrant, excited
Andrew Ganz. We have been told in no uncertain terms that
we are not to leave our seats or use our cell phones. We have

also been told not to discuss what we had seen on stage at the time of the murder until after the detective of record arrives. Good luck with that.

Also sitting in this section, but situated away from the rest of us, is Jake Barnes, the actor who plays Sweeney. He is sullenly staring at his hands, blood-stained from his close encounter with Andrew and manacled because he has been arrested. Two huge police officers are keeping him company because he did just kill a man. None of us believe that Jake killed knowingly; he seemed as surprised as everyone when he learned of the real razor he had held and Andrew's death. But I suppose that he could be acting. He was, after all, nominated for a Tony.

Members of the stage crew and Kate, the stalwart stage manager in charge of the crew, are still in their all-black attire and have been placed in the less padded and more cramped main floor seats. They sit toward the rear of the house, in the shadow of the rows of mezzanine seating that protrude above them. They were given the same instructions. We are, we assume, all suspects.

I figure this division of cast and crew is just a matter of convenience, to separate those on the stage and in the orchestra pit from those situated backstage. The thing is, theater artists have been deemed separate and apart from theater artisans ever since the ancient Greeks invented theater. Actors are the high-profile face of the production; crew members are faceless and pretty much invisible if they are doing their jobs well. And actors, not crew, get celebrated for their efforts at the end of a performance. During the first American Theatre Wing's Tony Award ceremony in 1947, the only non-performance people put up for recognition and invited to share in the chicken breast with black cherry sauce, brown rice, and asparagus tips were the costume designers. There's now a Tony for scenic design, lighting design, and sound design, but there is still no Tony Award for stage management.

So for the *Sweeney Todd* stage crew, being suspected of murdering Andrew Ganz takes a back seat to, well, the insult of being placed in the back seats.

The ushers have verified that no one left their seats after returning from intermission, so audience members are now being released after showing their ticket stubs and IDs, which the police record. There was no way anyone in the audience had access to the backstage area at the time of Andrew's murder. On the way out of the theater, ticket holders are given the name and phone number of a trauma specialist and notified that a detective will most likely be calling as a follow-up, should any valuable information come to mind.

Those in attendance who are affiliated with the front office of the North Coast Theater company are being detained a little longer and asked for a statement before being released. This includes the public relations team, who will have their hands full spinning what occurred and dealing with the dazed, but still-driven critics waiting for them outside the doors of the theater.

A few members of the cast, crew, and audience are being attended to by the medical unit that came with the police. They were all injured—bumps and bruises, mostly—while rushing to Andrew's side as he lay on the stage after the stage manager called "halt." One after the other, they slipped on the trail of blood that poor Andrew left in his wake. According to several of the actors who were watching from the wings and did not, themselves, feel compelled to help, the good Samaritans all flew heels-over-head like vaudevillian slapstick comedians, but without the hilarious ascending slide whistle sound effect upon their elevation. Nor was there the uproarious rim shot percussion hit upon their hard landing.

A rather freaked-out Gwen, who is also being attended to, sits on the edge of the thrust stage wrapped in blankets to offer her some comfort and to cover up the gruesome reminders she wears of the murder that occurred. She smiles at me when our eyes meet to indicate that she is OK. I give her an awkward thumbs-up to signal the same and point pathetically at the little bandage that was put on my neck by a medic to indicate how thankful I am that all I received from Sweeney's blade was a nick. But it is clear that we are both pretty rattled from what we experienced.

Unable to discuss the evening's events among themselves, the group of actors decide to tell stories about other theater folks who had died on stage.

Sure, this is not your normal response to the gruesome death of a colleague. But actors are not particularly normal in the best of times. Plus, dopamine is still rattling in our brains from performing, adrenaline is pumping in our veins from the drama that followed, and we are being suspected of murder. We need a creative outlet.

"I remember hearing about a community theater actress who died while performing in the old melodrama *The Drunkard* at the Towson Moose Lodge in Baltimore," began Charlie Mathias, a long-time North Coast Theater company member. He plays Judge Turpin, the fellow who falsely imprisoned a younger Sweeney Todd, ravaged his wife, and took his daughter Johanna as his ward and future bride. Charlie tends to play romantic leads, what with his rugged good looks and athletic six-foot, five-inch frame. But he's a very convincing bad guy in our production.

Given all that happened this evening, he is remarkably upbeat. Particularly so for a guy who was scheduled for a shave from Sweeney later in Act II. Actors!

"Edith Webster was her name," he continues. "The sixty-year-old amateur player sang a lively little ditty—ironically titled, 'Please Don't Talk About Me When I'm Gone'—and had a sudden heart attack upon its conclusion." Charlie pulls the opening lyric of the song from memory with the aid of a few notes from the clarinetist sitting two rows behind him. The two are about to start a second verse when they are stared at and effectively shut down by several uniformed officers who were clearly not fans of musical theater.

"When the actress face-planted onto the floor after the song," resumes a more subdued Charlie, as we all lean in to better hear the story, "the audience thought it was part of the show and gave her a rousing round of applause. When she didn't respond, the audience thought she was just milking the moment, and rewarded her showmanship with a standing ovation." Our laughter warrants another stern look from the officers as well as daggers from the eyes of the stage crew at the back of the theater, who are sitting silently and stoically as requested by the authorities and per their stealth training and Jedi discipline.

"Not a lot of people know this," adds Silvia Cooper, our meat pie-slinging Mrs. Lovett, in a clever attempt to weave implausible fiction into possible fact, "but the theater critic from the *Towson News-Herald Gazette Times Courier* was also the small-town newspaper's obit writer. With only limited column inches at his disposal, he merged his review with a memorial. It read: 'Known for her remarkable realism and flair for improvisation on stage, Edith Webster didn't disappoint in last night's *The Drunkard*. Her next appearance will be a matinee at the Murphy Funeral Home this Saturday, with visiting hours from 10 a.m. to 3 p.m.'" We all clap, quietly, in appreciation of Silvia's ingenuity.

Sitting this close to her under the intense emergency house lights, and with her long black hair still piled on the top of her head in a disheveled Mrs. Lovett coiffure, I can easily see the tell-tale black outlines of Silvia's tattoos despite the flesh-colored stage make-up covering them. They depict the detailed heads of infamous female villains in Shakespeare's plays who, not unlike Mrs. Lovett herself, are unbothered by the prospect of killing people. The insane Lady Macbeth, who conspires to kill the king, is on the nape of her neck. The vengeful Tamora from *Titus Andronicus,* in which fourteen characters die, is associated with barbarism, savagery, and unrestrained lasciviousness. She is on Silvia's well-defined right tricep while the ruthless Queen from *Cymbeline*, known as the master of manipulation, is on her left. The artwork is impressive, as must be Silvia's pain threshold and affection for the macabre.

Another actor chimes in with a similarly inappropriate and invented review of *The Drunkard* and Edith Webster's role in it had the theater critic also been the paper's sports columnist: "Going, going, gone!"

"'In tribute to Edith Webster,'" says another actor as if reading an obituary written by the theater critic who is also the paper's weather correspondent, "'The Towson Moose Lodge stage will be dark tonight with a continued chance of darkness into the morning.'" This is met with good-natured groans.

Unable to resist looking at the drop cloth-covered body still on the stage and being brutally reminded of life's capriciousness, I come up with something clever had the *Towson News-Herald Gazette Times Courier* theater critic also been the paper's self-help columnist: "Dear Perturbed: So you think you've got problems."

Before I can share it, all heads abruptly swivel toward the emergency exit closest to the stage at the far left of the theater as the heavy double doors slam open with a bang. They make way for two huge figures who, we assume, are the detective and what appears to be her pet yeti.

Chapter 6

Where's the Critic?

I'M DETECTIVE BRANDSTÄTTER. Where's the critic?" asks this force of nature to no one in particular. She enters the house of the theater with stone-cold serious intent, an all-business expression on her face, and an intimidating physicality. It is immediately clear who is in charge.

Her voice has no problem carrying because of the stunned silence her dramatic entrance created. But Detective Brandstätter obviously has years of experience being heard above the din of angry crowds, hungry members of the press, and too many dismissive male colleagues at closed-door meetings.

She looks like the outcome of experimental crossbreeding between an Amazon warrior and Arnold Schwarzenegger, which simultaneously attracts and repulses.

At the top of her tall torso is a large, chiseled head with perfectly symmetrical, somewhat Paleolithic facial features framed by flowing, jet-black hair. But the first thing I notice, even from this distance, is how her over-developed musculature—which makes itself known at the broad shoulders, sculpted bust, massive upper arms, and thick thighs—is squeezed into her otherwise well-fitting, off-the-rack gray pantsuit. Everything on her is hard, protruding, and screams World Wrestling Federation headliner. It is not difficult to imagine her tag-teaming the Sasquatch at her side and pile-driving bad guys.

"Did I stutter?" demands the detective, which sounds like a catchphrase from a *Terminator* film. "Where's the critic?"

In an involuntary response triggered by the alarming presence and proximity of unadulterated authority, quaking pointer fingers attached to every actor, musician, stage crew member, and red-coated usher are immediately aimed at me.

"No, the bloody one," she demands, and my pointer finger immediately aims at Gwen.

With a nod toward poor Gwen, but with her eyes still focused on me, the detective releases her huge assistant, who lumbers toward the quivering girl sitting on the edge of the stage. As he comes closer, I recognize the outdated, overburdened brown suit and the fellow in it.

My friend Larry is a soft-spoken, lovable giant of a man and a UC Berkeley-educated therapist specializing in trauma. He owns one suit—sadly, this one—preferring to private-practice his craft in baggy sweaters woven by his ex-wife from what looks like the matted fur of woolly mammoths. It is through his ex, who was a college roommate of my wife, Patty, that we met Larry.

He and a date, along with Patty and a few other friends, acquaintances, and work colleagues, were here to see me in the show's opening night performance. Actually, Larry is a big fan of musicals in general and Sondheim's musicals in particular, so it's fair to say that he was here to see *Sweeney Todd*.

Larry has consulted with the Cleveland police in the past, and I remember him mentioning a daunting, larger-than-life female detective and her no-nonsense approach to crime-solving, which nicely complemented his gentle nature. This has to be her for, surely, there cannot be two. He either asked if he could be of professional assistance, since he was already at the crime scene, or someone on the force recognized him in the crowd and asked him to lend a hand.

On his way to attend Gwen, Larry veers toward me to ask if I am OK and say that he will check in on me and Patty later in the evening. "This might take a while," he says, and adds in a whisper, "You were great in the show." Upon realizing that he might be hurting other actors' feelings, the ever-sentient Larry adds, "You were all great" and gives a quick wave to the sulking stage crew—who are caught off-guard and wave back—before giving his undivided attention to "the bloody one" in the blankets.

While Larry attends Gwen, I can see Detective Brandstätter consulting with several uniformed officers to no doubt coordinate whom she wants to talk to and in what order. After a few minutes, she leaves through the unmarked stage door that leads to the backstage area, and a few minutes after that, Larry leads Gwen out of the auditorium for a little private therapy.

I wouldn't mind a little therapy myself right about now, and not just for having witnessed a homicide set to a musical theater soundtrack. I just had my castmates call me out and turn me in without a moment's hesitation. I've got to imagine that George Plimpton probably didn't get a whole lot of love from the Lions, the Bruins, or boxing great Archie Moore either.

But I had thought that the cast and I created a genuine sense of community. It took a while, but after weeks together in rehearsals and performances of *As You Like It* and the first wave of performances of *Sweeney Todd* in Taos, we were a pretty close-knit theater family by the time we returned to Cleveland. Except for this whole murder thing.

But you don't have to look much farther than any murder mystery ever written to learn two evergreen truths about how close-knit families behave when a corpse unexpectedly floats to the surface at the lakefront ancestral property: Those who share the same blood tend to protect each other and those who marry into the family—like me joining this established theater company—are the first to be thrown under the bus.

Dear Perturbed: So you think you've got problems.

Chapter 7

Has Anyone Seen Freddie?

AFTER AN HOUR and a half of waiting in our seats under adult supervision, *Sweeney Todd's* director, Michael Price—a very talented man who hails from tiny Cahersiveen in County Kerry, looks as if he earned his degree in directing at Trinity College in Dublin on a rugby scholarship, and lives in NYC—is the first witness and potential suspect to be called backstage to be grilled by Detective Brandstätter.

He stands, gives us all a half-hearted wave with his fingers as he works his way across his row of seats with the grace of a seasoned thespian and the self-assuredness of a former athlete, and starts down the aisle. After a few steps, he stops, looks back at all of us, and says with a wide grin that lights up his ruddy complexion, "Hey, don't kill anyone else while I'm gone."

As if an afterthought, he looks around the room and adds, "Has anyone seen Freddie?" before continuing his journey. His Irish accent adds an extra layer of foreboding to the question, as if "Has anyone seen Freddie?" was the opening line of dialogue in Brian Friel's haunting play *Dancing at Lughnasa* or the final line in Conor McPherson's eerie *The Weir*.

Freddie Muñoz is a skinny, baby-faced ensemble member whose turn in Sweeney's barber chair was taken by Andrew Ganz. We have been so preoccupied with Andrew's murder and the chaos that followed that none of us thought about what had become of Freddie. After Michael pointed out his absence, everyone retreats into their personal space to quietly ponder the possibilities, none of them pleasant.

Since Freddie and I are ensemble players and in all the same scenes, we spend plenty of time together on stage, and he is probably the cast member I hang out with the most offstage.

Just before the "Johanna" number when Andrew was killed, we played drunk patrons of the meat pie shop during the "God, That's Good!" musical number at the top of Act II. At this point in the play, the pie shop is a going concern since Mrs. Lovett and Sweeney Todd have come up with a renewable source of protein—local Londoners—for the pies. About half-way through this huge production number, Freddie and I stumble offstage and do a quick costume change in separate, temporary backstage changing booths that were constructed just off the wings for immediate access.

After changing, Freddie walks up the wooden ramp closest to the changing booths and, unseen by the audience, takes his position on the stage right platform. There he awaits his cue to enter the barbershop in the dark before "Johanna" begins and sit in the chair as the first customer. After I change my costume, I cross backstage, walk up the ramp, and take my position on the stage left platform to anxiously await my cue to enter as the second customer.

Exiting the stage during "God, That's Good!", with Freddie's arm around my shoulder, was the last time I saw him. That was now about two hours ago. He's a sweet kid. Still, I've got to imagine that we are both prime suspects, what with our access to the barbershop at the time of the murder. Freddie's sudden disappearance does not bode well for his innocence.

Twenty minutes after Michael was summoned, stage manager Kate—who is short and stout, like a cast-iron fire hydrant, and has jaw-length indigo-dyed hair—is asked to follow a particularly lanky policeman backstage to where the detective is waiting. This creates a sight gag that is not lost on the actors and musicians watching them leave. It's not lost on the stage crew, either, but they are too allied as a unit and too committed to Kate to find humor in any one member's idiosyncrasies.

Twenty minutes after that, our Sweeney Todd is beckoned, and the officer who calls his name informs the rest of us that we are free to go. "You should expect a phone call or a visit from Detective Brandstätter or someone from her office," he says. He adds that management from North Coast Theater will be in touch in the morning to discuss tomorrow night's show and remaining performances.

Everyone stands to leave and the room gets loud with expressions of relief and remorse. That is, until the officer says, "You . . . stay" to me and me alone, and then the room turns silent. With all eyes on me—most reflecting concern, some shock, and a few, vindication—I say the only thing that seems appropriate for this moment: "What the fuck?!"

Chapter 8

The Interrogation

A s THE CAST AND crew head through the stage door that leads backstage and to the dressing rooms, I sit in my chair thinking about why I've been summoned and trying to get my rapid heart rate and overactive imagination under control with a few deep breaths.

I also devise a rock-solid alibi in my head in preparation for its delivery to Detective Brandstätter: "I really didn't know Andrew Ganz that well and had nothing against him to warrant his demise. I have no idea who would. I was standing offstage on a platform before the murder, like I do every night, visible to any actor or crew member who had business in that part of the performance space. I was busy thinking through the steps of my entrance and my fall down the trap, and not paying any attention to anyone or anything happening anywhere at any time."

After about twenty minutes, I am summoned and escorted backstage. My freaked-out mind expects a long, slow walk deep into the bowels of the nearly one-hundred-year-old Hedley Theatre through a damp, subterranean catacomb where our footsteps echo off the cold stone floor and into a dark and isolated room that awaits us at the dead-end of the hallway. And I envision my escort playing good cop to Detec-

tive Brandstätter's bad cop—which I imagine she is great at—
in order to break my spirit and sweat the truth out of me. So
my game is thrown off a bit when we just take a short walk
down the dimly lit hall and make an immediate right turn
into the plush greenroom where we actors hang out backstage
before the show and during intermission.

The brightness of the fluorescent lights is momentarily dis-
orienting, and the framed posters on the white walls—with
their wildly exaggerated images from recent North Coast
Theater productions of Ira Levin's *Deathtrap,* Stephen King's
Misery, and Shakespeare's *Julius Caesar*—seem particularly
surreal, oddly relevant to my current situation, and disturbing, given my confused state of mind.

Tasty albeit picked-through opening night snacks provided
by management—assorted raw vegetables and dip, yellow
cheese cubes, and miniature meat pies—are still available on
a circular table. Gorgeous flowers from well-wishers, which
add a sweetness to the omnipresent smell of Febreze and oil-
based stage makeup in the air, are scattered around the room
in vases. Not quite what I expected for an interrogation.

A relaxed Detective Brandstätter is sitting on one of the
overstuffed purple couches with her suit jacket off, her shirt
sleeves rolled up, and a napkin with some snacks balanced
on her lap. My therapist friend Larry walks in just after me,
holding a bottle of scotch and three glasses. With his foot, he
closes the door behind him to give us privacy and help negate
the sound of actors talking while walking down the hall to the
theater lobby to make their long-anticipated exit.

"Take a seat, Asher," mumbles the detective with a mouth-
ful of meat pie.

As I do, the rehearsed alibi in my head cascades out of my
mouth without warning or provocation. I am well aware that
I am blabbering and sounding panicky and disingenuous, as

if the role of Asher Kaufman is being played by Peter Lorre doing a bad imitation of Edward G. Robinson poorly impersonating Humphrey Bogart in a second-rate film noir flick. "You've got nothing on me, Coppers. I'm innocent, see. Innocent." It is pretty clear to everyone that I had never been in a situation like this before. Larry watches in dumbfounded amazement bordering on amusement.

"Try and relax, Asher," says the detective, as she finishes off the meat pie. "I know it's been a tough night."

Shaking my head to clear it and nervously picking at the edge of the bandage on my neck, I mutter, "Do I need a lawyer?"

"We only have three glasses, but I could get another," says Larry with a wry smile on his double-wide face. He puts the glasses down on the table between us and pours about two huge fingers worth of scotch into each, explaining that Johnny Walker Red was all they had at the convenience store just down the street from the theater.

"It's hard to find single malt in a bodega at midnight," admits the detective as she takes a glass and reaches out to hand it to me. "You're not a suspect. I'm off duty. Let's chat."

My friend takes a seat on the same couch as the detective, which audibly groans upon its reluctant acceptance of his bulk. "Easy there, big guy," I remark, starting to feel a bit more like myself or, at least, trying to sound that way. "We're going to need that couch for the rest of the run."

Detective Brandstätter tells me that Larry, who is now happily leaning into his glass of scotch, is someone she has worked with on several occasions, both as a trauma specialist and as someone well-schooled in criminal psychology. "I've learned to trust him without reservation," she adds, "and I tend to trust no one."

"They call me 'The Priest' at the downtown precinct," says

Larry, who is pouring himself a refill, "because I inspire confessions."

"We call him 'The Priest' because he always wears the same suit to work," says the detective, whose sense of humor, I have since learned, is remarkably dry and emerges with the same infrequency as cicadas.

"You should know that Larry explained why you are in this play, vouched for your integrity, and made a good argument for your innocence regarding Andrew Ganz, which is good enough for me." I have no doubt that she will be checking me out anyway, along with all the other persons of interest connected to Andrew.

She also says that she wants to talk with me because I had the best seat in the house during the murder. "Your colleague Gwen had the second-best seat in the house, since Ganz nearly landed in her lap, but she's in shock and Larry sent her home. You're a theater critic, so you're a trained observer. I've got some questions about what you observed."

I finish off my scotch, as does the detective, and she grabs the bottle to refill our glasses without taking her eyes off me. It is a generous pour and an intense gaze.

"Let me tell you what I know," she says, "and I'd like for you to tell me what I don't. Are you up for that?"

"Will I get a cool nickname, like Larry's?"

Larry smiles at this sign that I am coming back from wherever I went, emotionally, in the aftermath of the murder.

"Let's not get ahead of ourselves," says the detective, as she reaches over and takes a notepad and pencil out of her coat pocket. Her phone rings, which she answers, and says that her forensics team has showed up to go over the crime scene. "I'll be back," she utters as she stands and turns to leave the room.

As soon as she is out of sight, I burst out laughing at these particular words coming out of the mouth of a female

Schwarzenegger, look at Larry, and he bursts out laughing as well. I feel bad finding humor at the detective's expense, and Larry feels terrible laughing during an evening of horrific tragedy. But if Detective Brandstätter had said, "Hasta la vista, Baby!" I'm sure we both would have peed ourselves.

Chapter 9

Because It's a Comedy

D ETECTIVE BRANDSTÄTTER IS a brilliant crime solver," says
Larry as we await her return and, while waiting, go about
drinking what remains of the scotch. "But she is completely
out of her element where plays and actors are concerned.
She's a classic workaholic whose only form of refuge is the
gym. Before we entered the theater, she very reluctantly asked
me if there was an insider I knew who could serve as a liaison,
be an interpreter, and be discreet, and I recommended you."

"You know as much about theater as I do," I tell him. But
Larry admits that while he knows about shows, he has no idea
how they go from page to stage. "You're the guy on the front
line."

After conferring with her forensics team, the detective
returns to the greenroom, takes her seat, and is ready to get
down to business.

"Larry is convinced that whoever murdered Andrew Ganz
did it on stage and on opening night to make a very public
statement. Or, more disturbingly, just to have an audience,"
she says to me as she thumbs through her notes. "But North
Coast Theater, with this same cast and crew, staged *As You Like
It* before *Sweeney Todd*. Any idea why someone didn't try to kill
Ganz on the opening night of *As You Like It*?"

I think about this for a moment, but the cobwebs in my

head have not fully vanished since Andrew's execution, and the scotch isn't helping. So clarity and caution are not really on the menu this evening, though I am feeling incredibly chatty.

"Because it's a comedy?"

The detective looks at me for a hard moment, trying to figure out if I am serious, still in shock, or a smart-ass. I was being serious, but the detective seems to be leaning toward smart-ass. She then looks over at Larry, as if second-guessing his choice for a consultant.

"You know," he interjects, "about 155 of Shakespeare's characters die in his plays."

"My take-away from this is what, Larry?" asks the detective.

"No one dies in any of his comedies. Asher is right about *As You Like It* not being the right setting for a murder. It's a comedy about love and rejuvenation. *Sweeney Todd* is all about corruption, desire, and vulgarity. Judge Turpin lusts after the girl he has brought up as his daughter. Mrs. Lovett yearns for Sweeney and is willing to forget about what's right and wrong to attract him. Todd, who is driven by emotion, wants to do nothing but kill. Maybe our killer does, as well, which is why this musical was selected."

"In *As You Like It*," I add, "Shakespeare writes that everyone is 'exempt from public haunt, finds tongues in trees, books in the running brooks, sermons in stones, and good in everything.' Hardly the place for a murder. That was the point I was trying to make. Earlier. When you asked."

"I don't think a murderer would care about such things," says the detective dismissively.

"A murderer who is into theater—who knows both these shows—might," I suggest and Larry nods in agreement, which seems to win over Detective Brandstätter. At least temporarily.

"And," I add, "the *Sweeney Todd* script actually calls for a character to be standing center stage wielding a sharp object and putting it to the throat of another character."

"There's no lethal weapon in *As You Like It*?"

"Just the characters' rapier wit," I say with a smile.

"I'm starting to get some ideas for your nickname," sighs the detective.

While the detective and I are conversing, Larry is scanning the list of musical numbers in a *Sweeney Todd* playbill that is laying on the table. "The murder took place during the 'Johanna' song," he says. "But it was during the Act II reprise and not when the song was sung twice—let's see, first by the good-guy character Anthony Hope, and then by the bad-guy character Judge Turpin—back in Act I. That's kind of interesting."

A thought pops into my head, which I can't help but share.

"Just after intermission and right before the reprise of 'Johanna' is a song called 'God, That's Good!' It's actually a huge production number that involves all of us ensemble members. There's also—let's see—Sweeney, Mrs. Lovett, her young assistant Tobias, and some of the show's other featured actors who we have disguised as local Londoners so they can help fill out the ensemble and add their voices to the song. It's a complicated number that also involves the entire crew—lots of props coming in and out with set pieces that need to be rotated. Backstage would be empty with all this happening on stage. Could intermission and 'God, That's Good!' be an opportunity to set up a murder that didn't exist for the earlier versions of 'Johanna?'"

Larry scans the playbill and confirms that there is nothing right before the Act I renditions of "Johanna" that could clear the backstage area or give a murderer time and room to operate without being seen.

With that, Detective Brandstätter takes the playbill from Larry, grabs a pen, and circles something in the middle pages.

"Earlier, I had a talk with your director and stage manager about what was happening backstage just before the murder. They both mentioned that 'God, That's Good!' had just ended. I asked them to identify who was not engaged during that number. I've circled the headshots of those actors. No one involved in this production is being ruled out until we do background checks to see if anyone in the cast or crew has cause, but these are the people who had the opportunity."

She looks at me for a moment as if questioning the wisdom of what she's about to ask. She asks it anyway, in the form of a declaration, while passing me the playbill.

"I'd like for you to take this home and think about these people. Think about whether there was anything you may have seen or heard during rehearsals or backstage tonight that could be relevant. Meet me back here in the morning to continue this discussion. I'll also want you to walk me through those two musical numbers, from before and during the murder."

I nod as I flip through the playbill's cast list and stare at the circled faces of seven friends. I must have looked like I had something to say because Larry asks if there's a problem. There is. I had noticed that Freddie's head shot was not circled, even though he went AWOL, and, like me, had direct access to the barbershop just before the murder. I hold up the playbill to Detective Brandstätter and point at Freddie's postage stamp-sized black-and-white photo.

"After the show was stopped and before I arrived on the scene," she explains, "I phoned in and asked an officer to accompany several ushers backstage to get the cast and crew to move into the house and take a seat. One of those ushers found Muñoz, dead, in one of the quick-change booths. We're investigating two murders. I'll see you back here at 10 a.m."

Chapter 10

Art Imitating Life

FROM THE EDITOR: This is the second in a series of behind-the-scenes articles by critic Asher Kaufman about his adventures in North Coast Theater's production of *Sweeney Todd*. The show is currently in technical rehearsal in Taos, New Mexico, and opens in Cleveland in four weeks.

I shared my lunch today with Anita Sánchez, North Coast Theater's veteran dramaturg. She's a theater historian by training and her task here is to help keep our staging of *Sweeney Todd*—the production values and the performances—in the 19th century.

Over a homemade tuna salad sandwich and store-bought chips, I learn that the character Sweeney Todd is based on an urban legend about an actual barbarous barber who murdered his clients. The tale was popularized in a series of short stories in 1846 that appeared in a cheap London publication. The rag specialized in supposedly real melodramatic horror tales, which were all the rage at the time.

"So," she says, "to some extent, our Sweeney Todd is an eerie example of art imitating life."

The first play version of the Todd story, I am told, was penned by someone other than the short story author and appeared on stage a year after the published tales. It was eventually turned into a silent movie—penned by someone else—that opened in British theaters in 1928. The Sondheim musical, which opened on Broadway in 1979, was based on a version of the story that was written by an English playwright in 1973.

"So," she continues, "art also imitates art. And in the process, over time, we lose track of the fact that at the heart of the Sweeney Todd story is actual mayhem, actual murder, and actual misery. And part of my job is to make sure that element is not lost—that everything about our production rings true."

She is doing her job well. Thus far in the rehearsal process, great attention to detail is being given to make the murdering as realistic as possible. The original Broadway production was a big-picture masterpiece that, according to one review, placed the show's luridness "in a distancing Dickensian social framework." Our production brings that luridness claustrophobically close.

I expect that our audiences will be as entertained by the story as they are shocked by the realism of our story-telling.

Chapter 11

Little Beadle Bamford

Aᴼᴛᴇʀ ɪ ᴄʜᴀɴɢᴇ out of my costume—which I have managed to sweat through completely given tonight's performance and scotch-infused interrogation with Detective Brandstätter—Larry and I leave the theater through the stage door in the rear and find his car in the now-vacant patron parking lot. A text I received from my wife, Patty, lets me know that she was aware of my detention and left hours ago. She offered Larry's date a ride and writes that she's worried about me and will be awake when I get home.

I scrape a thin layer of ice off the windshield—the first real sign that fall is transitioning into an early Cleveland winter—and I'm doing the driving. Despite his mass, Larry is a lightweight when it comes to alcohol. I feel fine, but if I start swaying or speeding, I've got the detective's get-out-of-jail-free business card in my shirt pocket.

I'll drop Larry off at his house and Uber home.

We sit in silence for a while. Larry's eyes are closed and mine are on the lookout for black ice on the asphalt of the empty city streets leading to the entry ramp for the highway that will take us to the eastern suburbs and home. My mind is reeling from all that happened this evening. Craziest opening night ever.

"Sorry about the loss of your theater friends," says Larry. "You OK?"

"I guess. Thanks. Oh, Patty brought home your friend, in case you were wondering. Quite the memorable first date. It will be a hard one to top."

"It will be our romantic go-to story when we are married, old, and gray," murmurs Larry with his eyes still closed. "'Hey, Honey, remember our first date when there was that double homicide and then I abandoned you at the theater?' Our song will be 'Worst Pies in London' and we'll name our children Sweeney, Lovett and Tobias."

"And Beadle Bamford."

"Ah, he's the needy, evil sidekick of Judge Turpin who does all his dirty work. A good name for a middle child who is always craving attention and getting into mischief. Little Beadle Bamford."

"What's your date's name?"

"No idea," says a somewhat inebriated Larry.

More silence. More driving.

"The Priest? Really?"

"What can I say?" mumbles Larry, with half-asleep exuberance. "I am the master of criminal psychology. I inspire confessions. It's a gift," he says with a yawn.

"I have a confession."

"See?!"

"I wish you hadn't vouched for me. I'd so much rather be a suspect for a crime I didn't commit than be Dr. Watson to Detective Brandstätter's, well, Detective Brandstätter. I'd be home already, in bed and asleep. Plus, I didn't see anything. And this is my theater family I'm expected to rat out. Like being a critic in the cast wasn't hard enough."

"Your being a critic is exactly what the detective is counting on," says a reawakening Larry. "What happened tonight with

Ganz was very much a well-orchestrated performance staged before a select audience. So review it."

"Uh . . . no."

"Come on! How well was tonight's play-within-a-play orchestrated? Why all the drama of an onstage execution and a backstage murder? Which one of the seven actors circled in the playbill would be best cast as the murderer?"

"No. And by the way, you told the detective that *Sweeney Todd* is a case study of corruption and desire. If anything, *Sweeney Todd* is a case study of revenge. The title character is blinded by it. Revenge is what drives this musical."

"You're great at this!"

"No."

"Maybe revenge is what drives Ganz's and Muñoz's murderer," declares Larry, now fully awake and in full therapist mode. "You could be right—this whole thing may be about revenge. Perhaps something in the actors' brief bios in the playbill will speak to you."

"Actors list roles in past productions, the name of the school they graduated from, and the people they want to thank for their success. Unless an actor made a career out of traveling the country playing Third Murderer in random productions of *Macbeth*, graduated from Joliet rather than Julliard, and thanks Satan for his guidance, I don't think much will come from playbill bios. Look, I'm the wrong guy for this. And it's too soon. And I'm tired."

"The detective really needs your help, or she never would have asked for it. She thought *Sweeney Todd* was an opera, for God's sake, and she'll never figure out that whole upstage/downstage and stage right/stage left thing. She finds people singing and dancing to express their emotions genuinely disturbing."

Again, silence.

"Do you remember the last time I was your plus-one at a show?" asks Larry. "You were reviewing the Great Lakes Theater production of some famous murder mystery?"

"That was *And Then There Were None*, which was based on the old Agatha Christie novel."

"Five minutes into the play, you leaned over and casually told me who you thought the murderer was, and, of course, you were right. Ruined the whole evening for me, but that was some brilliant deduction. Just do what you did for *And Then There Were None* with *Sweeney Todd*."

"Here's another confession. I knew who the murderer was in the play because I had read the novel."

"Ah. Well, then, good luck tomorrow."

Chapter 12

And Are You Beautiful and Pale with Yellow Hair

Iᴛ's ʟᴀᴛᴇ ʙʏ the time the Uber driver drops me at home after this harrowing opening night. I check in on the sleeping twelve-year-old Zoey and sixteen-year-old Austin in their bedrooms, the sleeping Patty in our bedroom, and go into the kitchen to ponder, over leftovers, the playbill Detective Brandstätter gave me.

Just as I empty my pockets and put their contents on the kitchen counter, my phone vibrates with an incoming text from Larry: "Hey, remembered the name of my date—Christine—and called her to apologize for not taking her home myself. She reminded me of something weird we both heard during the play. Probably nothing, but let's talk. Call my office tomorrow, since I have a full day of patients, and I'll get back to you ASAP. I think I'll call your colleague Gwen in the morning, just as a professional courtesy, and follow up. Tough night, Asher. Hope you get some rest."

After heating up a plate of the chili and bean casserole I made last night that was mediocre the first time around, I flip through the first few pages of advertising in the playbill on my way to the cast bios and come to the names and titles of all the people who manage the North Coast Theater company.

At the top of the food chain is Andrew Ganz, whose picture and title of producing artistic director is the most prominently displayed. The title means that Andrew has the overarching artistic control of the troupe's production choices, directorial choices, and overall artistic vision.

Anyone pissed off about marketing, institutional advancement, educational services, community outreach, contract negotiation, or human resources would likely kill the theater's managing director, whose name appears just below Andrew's.

Here's the thing. Everyone on the artistic side of this production owes a debt of gratitude to Andrew Ganz.

He hired them or signed off on the director's and musical director's decision to hire them. And he hired the director and musical director. He hired me.

Plus, he's a genuinely nice guy who pretty much lives his job, which takes him from Cleveland to Taos and back again with great frequency throughout the year's production schedule. I've been covering North Coast Theater for years and I have never heard anything about sex scandals, harassment issues, political power plays, or personality conflicts. Andrew's been a champion of gender- and color-blind casting and an advocate of placing actors who identify as LGBTQ+ in roles that are LGBTQ+. That can't be said with such assuredness for most other professional theater companies in Cleveland.

The majority of North Coast's company members and most of the crew, including the stage manager and dramaturg, have worked under Andrew for years. Everyone seems happy and secure in what they do.

So who would want Andrew Ganz dead? And why Freddie, as well?

I start reading the bios below each circled face of an actor and expect to find nothing. In fact, the first of the seven—

which belongs to Erin Andrews—specifically thanks the artistic director.

ERIN ANDREWS (Johanna in *Sweeney Todd*/Celia in *As You Like It*). Four seasons with North Coast Theater. Favorite roles with the company include Cosette in *Les Misèrables* and Yvette in *Clue: The Musical*. Made her theatrical debut at eleven as Johanna in the Stagedoor Manor theater camp production of *Sweeney Todd, Jr.: School Edition*. Erin would like to thank Andrew Ganz for supporting her talents with so many artistic opportunities. A proud SUNY Purchase grad, as well as a certified holistic health coach.

When I first met Erin at the theater company meet-and-greet before our first rehearsal, she was one of the few actors who didn't despise me—a critic in the cast—upon first contact. Quite the opposite. When she saw me from across the room, she pranced toward me as if on the verge of taking flight. The actress is a tiny, yellow-haired pixie straight out of *A Midsummer Night's Dream* with a huge singing voice.

Every encounter with her backstage and offstage has been nothing but delightful. She drinks alcohol-free lite beer at bars, which she never finishes, and gives unsolicited nutrition advice. She laughs easily and often. She hugs me and everyone in the cast before every performance. She hugs the crew. She adores her wife, Silvia, who is our heavily tatted Mrs. Lovett in *Sweeney Todd*, and Silvia adores her back.

I can't imagine Erin killing anyone, which, in most murder mysteries, is the very reason to suspect her big time. Too damn cute! And she wasn't on stage during "God, That's Good!"

But Erin clocks in at about five feet and barely a hundred pounds. Her arms and legs are toothpicks. She is physically incapable of overpowering Freddie and Andrew. And even if

Andrew were somehow rendered semi-conscious, she is physically incapable of dragging that tall drink of water up a ramp, across the barbershop in the dark, and into a chair.

I take the black Sharpie marker that's sticking out of a front pocket of Zoey's middle-school backpack on the kitchen counter, put a line through Erin's headshot without hesitation, and move on to the next circled face in the playbill.

Chapter 13

Showstopper

JAKE BARNES (Sweeney). North Coast Theater debut. A Tony Award nominee, whose Broadway credits include *Scandalous, In My Life, American Psycho, Spider-Man: Turn Off the Dark,* and *Bonnie & Clyde.* Many regional productions and much voiceover work. In 2014, Jake made his Metropolitan Opera debut in *The Death of Klinghoffer.* Training: Juilliard, Actor's Studio.

Though impressive on the surface, I know as a theater critic that Jake's Broadway experience consists largely of bombs. Remarkably so. *In My Life,* a long-shot to even make it to Broadway, lasted for only sixty-one performances. It was about a young man with Tourette's syndrome and brain cancer, and had such memorable lyrics as "There's a little rumor/Someone's got a tumor." According to Ben Brantley, the critic for *The New York Times,* "I found myself trapped inside a musical Hallmark card." He was kind enough not to even mention Jake in his review.

Scandalous, a musical about radio evangelist Aimee Semple McPherson, found Jake on stage in a minor role for twenty-nine performances. Said David Cote, who wrote for *Time Out New York* at the time, "I have seen worse shows, but few as wild-eyed and zealously wrongheaded." And, sadly, he does mention Jake. Only Jake's name was an unmemorable

Harvey Stone at the time. Not sure if the name change was an effort to distance himself from these unflattering notices, but I wouldn't doubt it.

The musical *American Psycho* closed after fifty-four performances. *Spider-Man*, a troubled enterprise from the get-go, lost $60 million by the time it closed—a Broadway record. "*Bonnie & Clyde* isn't the worst musical to open on Broadway in the past decade," noted *Wall Street Journal* critic Terry Teachout. "It is, however, quite sufficiently bad enough to qualify for the finals."

I'm not suggesting that Jake is single-handedly responsible for these short-lived productions, but he sure was in the room where it happened and is very much the poster child for the term "showstopper." And not in the good way. He certainly stopped the show during our *Sweeney Todd*.

Jake is an unknown entity in our cast. Unlike most of us, he was brought in from New York exclusively for *Sweeney Todd* and did not perform in *As You Like It*. As an outsider and a late arrival, he never got the chance to buddy-up with the others and didn't seem all that interested in doing so when he joined the cast.

Tackling him and landing on his chest during the opening night debacle was about as close as the two of us ever got, for Jake went through rehearsals as if there were a dark, menacing cloud following him overhead. His preshow preparation entailed isolation and pacing. I just attributed all this to him being a method actor, like Marlon Brando and Daniel Day-Lewis, and figured his being moody and often inaccessible was just him "becoming" Sweeney per the Meisner Approach or Uta Hagen Technique.

"But did becoming Sweeney include actually committing murder?" I say out loud, as if doing so would add objectivity to the accusation, like it was someone else's diabolical idea.

"What are you doing up so late at night?" says a sleepy Patty in pajamas, as she enters the kitchen, kisses my cheek, and takes a fork full of my leftovers. "Larry called a while ago to say that you were Ubering home from his place. Sorry I couldn't stay awake for you. Are you all right?"

I tell her that I am, and ask the same of her. I also tell her that the person in charge of the case, Detective Brandstätter, assigned me the new vocation of ace crime solver and the pay is a pending nickname. She sees the playbill on the table, the circled headshot of Jake Barnes, and lets out her signature laugh, which is airy, effortless, and infectious.

"What's funny about the photo?" I ask while laughing along with her.

"Not the photo. The name. I was just helping Austin with a book report," she says as she rummages through his school backpack and pulls out a ten-page essay in a plastic binder. "He's reading Ernest Hemingway in AP English and writing about the author's misogyny. Jake Barnes is the fictional character who narrates the story in the novel *The Sun Also Rises*. I never made that connection with the *Sweeney* actor before."

I flip through and read random sections of the essay, which also touch on characters in the short stories *Hills Like White Elephants* and *The Short Life of Francis Macomber*. I learn that the Jake Barnes character is an expatriate American living in Paris in the 1920s who has an injury suffered during World War I that has rendered him impotent. He's also a man who is prone to petty cruelty.

"Although Jake is a typical manly Hemingway hero in his mastery of trout fishing and his appreciation of bullfighting," concludes my son in the final paragraph with an inherited flair for hyperbole, "his insecurities about his masculinity are typical of the anxieties that many members of the Lost Generation felt. Including, perhaps, Hemingway himself."

"Yeah, I can't imagine the guy chose that name knowing its origin. It's just his professional moniker," I tell Patty. But I turn the page in the playbill and leave the circled headshot unaltered. After all, Jake—whether or not he actually possesses the sadomasochism shared by his namesake—did just kill a man.

Chapter 14

Mea Culpa

CHARLIE MATHIAS PLAYS the evil Judge Turpin, the character who ruined the life of Sweeney Todd. The actor, who has been with North Coast Theater company for nine seasons, thanks Jesus at the top of his brief bio. At the end he writes, "1 Corinthians 10:3." Could be killer code.

"Are you familiar with 1 Corinthians 10:3?" I ask Patty, who points to the Jewish symbol *chai* at the end of her necklace and returns my query with a deadpan stare. She takes my phone, looks up the passage at biblehub.com, and reads: "God always provides some way to avoid sin. So, they must avoid giving anyone the idea that they approve of idol worship, even by knowingly eating food offered to idols. Their first question must always be, 'Will this glorify God?'"

"Glorifying God is not something Charlie does openly," I say while staring down at his headshot. "At least not while he's on the job."

"I think he's become more faithful," notes Patty, as she takes the fork and digs into the casserole on my plate, "since the cancer returned. I've noticed that at cast parties."

Charlie was made aware of his pancreatic cancer's recurrence during *As You Like It*, where he played both Duke Frederick and Duke Senior. As his bio explains, he had routinely played leading men in North Coast Theater productions— William Gillette in *The Game's Afoot*, Fitzwilliam Darcy in *Pride and Prejudice*, the title role in *Hamlet*. Before joining North Coast Theater, he appeared as one of those gorgeous interns sleeping with all the other gorgeous interns in half a season of *Grey's Anatomy* before a bus that crashes into the hospital takes out his character. In his prime, he could have gone a few rounds with Detective Brandstätter and potentially held his own.

But what the detective didn't know when she circled his head shot was that at 7:25 p.m. at every performance of *As You Like It* and during the opening night performance of *Sweeney Todd*, the cast of sixteen formed a circle on the stage behind the closed curtain, held hands, and offered up some positive thoughts for Charlie. He got a kiss from everyone before we silently dispersed to take our places just before the curtain opened.

"Since we started the run of *Sweeney Todd*," I tell Patty, "Charlie has lost considerable weight and energy. Our costumer started putting shoulder padding in his Judge Turpin wardrobe and, when not on stage, he rests on the Equity cot that's been placed in the farthest temporary backstage changing booth, which actors know not to use during his brief respites. Crew members know where to find him before his next entrance." He has started wearing a splash of bay rum as well, not because his character does, but to cover up the distinctive odor of medicine and illness.

"He can't be a suspect," Patty declares in a whisper and on the verge of tears.

"No," I reply. "He can't."

Like Erin, Charlie isn't built for murder, physically or spiritually. I put a line through his circled headshot and Patty finds a red Sharpie marker in Zoey's backpack to add a small heart.

Chapter 15

Finishing the Casserole

MINUS THE HEART, I also put a line through the circled headshot of Justin Prentice, who plays Judge Turpin's sidekick and the namesake of Larry's unborn son. He's not a viable suspect.

JUSTIN PRENTICE (Beadle Bamford in *Sweeney Todd/* Amiens in *As You Like It*), is thrilled to experience his fifth season with North Coast Theater and the Taos Shakespeare Festival, where he has played Puck in *A Midsummer Night's Dream*, Marius in *Les Misèrables*, Simon Gascoyne in *The Real Inspector Hound*, and others. Professional credit highlights include Gala Concert—Stephen Sondheim's 75th Birthday, New Amsterdam Theater. BFA, Carnegie Mellon.

In addition to her not knowing about Charlie's illness, Detective Brandstätter doesn't know that Justin had been added to the meat pie-eating members of the ensemble in "God, That's Good!" He has one of the best voices in the cast, which goes under-utilized since Beadle is only in "Ladies in Their Sensitivities" with Judge Turpin in Act I and two brief novelty numbers, "Sweet Polly Plunklett" and "Tower of Bray," with Mrs. Lovett in Act II.

When rehearsals began for *Sweeney Todd*, the director had Justin singing from the wings during the large ensemble numbers he is not in. He was soon inserted into them, well disguised. This must have slipped Michael Price's mind when the director reviewed the cast list with Detective Brandstätter earlier this evening because I can't imagine the detective missing this.

Every night I see Justin sitting directly across from me, singing about meat pies. He was there tonight and was still on stage singing at the time Freddie and I stumbled offstage to do our quick costume change for the "Johanna" number. And, still in costume, he was one of the actors receiving medical attention after slipping on stage trying to give aid to the dying artistic director.

I put a line through his circled headshot and, while reaching over my shoulder, Patty turns the page, but not before she finishes off the casserole. She'll regret it when she wakes up in a few hours with indigestion, which will be fine with me, since I'm sure I'll be up all night second-guessing the innocence of my cast mates. I could use the company.

So far, Jake Barnes—our Sweeney—is the only viable suspect.

Chapter 16

Bars and Measures

THE NEXT PAGE opens to the circled face of Tony Silver, who plays the character Signor Adolfo Pirelli. "I love that character, and Tony did such a marvelous job with him tonight," says Patty, who is now warming up to the task at hand. "He was drunk, right?"

"Of course he was."

Pirelli is first introduced as a flamboyant Italian barber and tooth puller who has shaved kings and popes. But he is as fake as the hair growth elixir he sells on the London streets to naive customers. The conman was Sweeney Todd's apprentice as a boy, and now threatens to expose his former master's sordid history unless Todd shares his profits. Late in Act I, Todd kills Pirelli to keep his own identity a secret.

Tony has a remarkable singing voice, and he has made a career going from musical to musical and filling character roles that require his talents as a tenor. In fact, according to his bio, he has "played Pirelli in over two hundred performances in over a half-dozen productions of *Sweeney Todd* across the country, where he is required to sing a high operatic C5 without the benefit of falsetto."

But his highly animated facial features and his unique voice are too recognizable to be placed in any subsequent musical numbers in our production. Although he is not in "God,

That's Good!" he is most likely occupied elsewhere during that musical number if his track record holds true. During the run of *Sweeney Todd* in Taos, Tony was always at a bar across the street from intermission until the show's finale, when he would show up for curtain call reeking of gin. He already had botanical breath at the start of tonight's show.

I think he acts just to keep pace with his bar bills, which is not an uncommon occurrence among professional actors. Stories of Spencer Tracy, Peter O'Toole, and John Barrymore dance in my head.

"One phone call to local bartenders should remove Tony from the suspect list, right?" asks Patty.

"I'm confident that Tony was sitting on a new favorite bar-stool during the murder. He might be there still. But I guess he's a suspect until that phone call is made by the detective."

Chapter 17

Best Actor in a Non-Singing Role

BRANDON STEELE, WHO has been a North Coast Theater company member for four seasons, plays Jonas Fogg. Brandon is a viable suspect.

The character is a supporting antagonist and the corrupt head of the local insane asylum. He is in league with Judge Turpin, who keeps Johanna locked away in the asylum after hearing of her plan to elope with Anthony. Jonas Fogg, a small role, has the distinction of being the only character in the musical who does not sing or dance.

I spent a lot of time with Brandon during the production of *As You Like It*, since he was the kind young master Orlando to my old manservant Adam. There's nothing in his bio that raises flags, but the more I think about him, the more I recall some unpleasantries.

I remember when we were midway through the first week of rehearsals and all of the supporting actors arrived off book, most of the leading actors with volumes of dialogue were getting close, and I was still dependent on my script like an amateur. Iambic pentameter was kicking my ass. When we were running scenes, I could see Brandon impatiently mouthing my lines if there were a delay in me finding them on the page or getting them out of my mouth.

When I finally conquered my Shakespeare-speak, I remember stepping into the performance space for the first time without a script in my hands. I recall noticing that other actors in the rehearsal room had stopped what they were doing to watch. So did the crew. When I got through my scenes without a stumble, there were playful high fives and "Huzzahs" from everyone in the rehearsal room, but Brandon just stood by impatiently, eager to get on with the next scene.

"I never did like Brandon," says Patty, and she recalls telling me so at the downtown Cleveland restaurant where the closing night party for *As You Like It* was held. "I told you I found his All-American good looks and his overt awareness of his All-American good looks off-putting."

I have no memory of this discussion, but, then, I had spent most of that night at the dessert table eating my weight in miniature cream puffs, which I felt I richly deserved after surviving Shakespeare for eight performances a week for three weeks. I remember those cream puffs well, and could recognize them in a police lineup.

Being a temperamental professional and, perhaps, a bit of a bully does not make Brandon suspicious. Not being in the "God, That's Good!" number does, for it gives him the opportunity to engage in foul play, if he were so inclined. Plus, he can't be too happy going from a leading role in the previous play to a small, non-singing and non-dancing role in this one. And he can't be too happy with whoever made that decision.

Chapter 18

I Feel You, Johanna

CHRIS O'CONNELL, WHO is playing the clean-cut romantic lead, Anthony, is a suspect, as well. But only by circumstance.

He is a charming fellow. I don't know him well, and I spend very little time with him on stage, but he is always amiable and seems to be genuinely delighted to be a part of this production.

But before coming to North Coast Theater, after months of frustrating, fruitless Broadway auditions upon graduating from college, he took on work as a member of the entertainment crew on the Disney Cruise Line. I wrote about this in one of my behind-the-scenes pieces. Could he have been broken by the required perpetual smiling and the twenty-four-hours-a-day, seven-days-a-week of adorable? It sure would have broken me.

After a year-and-a-half at sea, Chris returned to tour the country in a mascot suit as the lovable title character Lyle, Lyle, Crocodile in a musical theater version of Bernard Waber's popular children's book. Is this the behavior of a sane man?

He has since settled into a career as an itinerant actor and musical theater gypsy with regional companies throughout the country. What is he running from?

Because the character Anthony kick-starts the "Johanna"

number with a solo at center stage, Chris' window of opportunity to get Andrew in the barber chair on the second level of the set piece and himself on the stage in time to hit his mark for the spotlight is extremely tight. I'll mention this to Detective Brandstätter in the morning.

"You seem to be finding fault with the ocean-going happiest-place-on-earth and a delightful children's book," says Patty, "which suggests that you are pretty fried from all that happened this evening." She takes the playbill from my hands, lays it on the table, and escorts me to the bedroom.

It takes several tries for my fingers to untie my shoes and undo the rest of my wardrobe, and the effort pretty much exhausts my resources. As I sit on the bed, random memories of the murder—the screaming, the blood trail on the stage, the audience standing in unison as they bear witness to Andrew's final strut and fret upon the stage—surge through my mind. When I lay down for a moment just to gather myself before I shower, as the bed caresses my body, my head touches down on the overstuffed pillow, and my thoughts trail off into non-sequiturs, I immediately lose consciousness.

Chapter 19

The Standing Ovation

FROM THE EDITOR: This is the third in a series of behind-the-scenes articles by critic Asher Kaufman about his adventures in North Coast Theater's production of *Sweeney Todd*. The show is currently in performance in Taos, New Mexico, and opens in Cleveland in two weeks.

I'm a big fan of the standing ovation. I think that watching live theater is a lot like watching a national basketball championship game, in that, win or lose, it is filled with lofty intentions, best efforts, and spontaneous heroics. Jumping to one's feet and, perhaps, storming the court is a natural response to those valiant exploits.

But it is important to be selective in one's standing in the theater. Too much standing renders the act valueless. To borrow a quote from the musical *Hamilton*, when the title character questions Aaron Burr's political commitment: "What do you stand for?"

According to several New York newspapers, the indiscriminate and automatic standing ovation is a pandemic that has befallen the professional stages of Broadway. This same thing is happening in London's West End. "It strikes me as nigh impossible that several hundred people can all have had that spontaneous urge and involuntarily leapt to their feet together," noted a befuddled theater critic for *The Independent* after witnessing the inevitable Standing O in action. He added, "Surely we can applaud Sir Kenneth Branagh and Dame Judi Dench from a seated position."

Word of ovation inflation has apparently not reached New Mexico. Last night, the sold-out opening night crowd at the Taos Shakespeare Festival loved our show and applauded loudly and appreciatively, but chose to stay in their seats.

It has been suggested that the rising cost of a ticket is responsible for rising audiences. Standing in applause helps convince ourselves that what we witnessed was worth the premium price of admission, that we actually had the kind of experience promised in the raving theater marquee quotes from critics.

Maybe the price point for a ticket in Taos is right on the money.

Cynics have stated that standing may be overcompensation for a lack of comprehension. Elevating after *In the Heights* or *Sponge Bob Square Pants*, they argue, will convince others that we "get it" and are cultural insiders, and not actually clueless when it comes to hip hop or hallucinogenic cartoons.

Perhaps our collective opening night audience was so Sondheim-savvy that it felt no great need to suggest otherwise by being seen standing.

Most of the professional actors in my cast, if asked, would say that serving the art and their fellow actors are the more meaningful outcomes of their craft. The rest would say that they are oblivious to audience response. And yet it was remarkably revealing—a personality litmus test of sorts—seeing their curtain call reactions as last night's audience stayed seated.

From the row behind the featured performers, I certainly noticed that some performers were gracious in their acceptance of whatever applause was offered. In fact, I saw our Beggar Woman and Tobias weeping in appreciation. But I could also see the white knuckles on the hands of our Mrs. Lovett as she clutched hard to keep from screaming, "Are you not entertained?!" to the perched patrons. I could hear the snide comments passing between our Jonas Fogg and Beadle Bamford, spoken with teeth clenched so the audience couldn't read their lips. Our Sweeney was so perturbed that his efforts went underappreciated that he only granted the audience one quick bow before dismissing the cast and storming off the stage.

They will love coming back to Cleveland, where audiences stand for everything. I've seen local audiences stand for scene changes.

A psychologist friend of mine suggested that this consumer behavior is leftover self-loathing from the Rust Belt city's historical inferiority complex. Standing is our way of subconsciously giving thanks to national tours and professional companies just for showing up at our theaters.

Clevelanders are standing because the theaters came awfully close to becoming parking lots not long ago, and have been recently renovated. They are applauding the $26 million restoration and transformation of the Allen Theatre, the $15.7 million renovation of the Hedley Theatre and, most of all, the $900,000 in improvements to the restrooms in the Ohio Theatre. They are standing to give thanks for the upgrade in peripheral signage, streetscape improvements, and the 20-foot-tall crystal chandelier that hangs outside the theaters at the hub of Playhouse Square.

For the sake of our apparently thin-skinned cast members, I hope those in attendance on the opening night of *Sweeney Todd* stand. Even if they are just applauding the chandelier.

Chapter 20

Twilight

IN THE MORNING, I awake after a solid night's sleep, and then shower. And by solid night's sleep, I mean deep, dreamless, and unsatisfying, as if my brain shut down, rather than dozed off. By shower, I mean cold water to help jump start my brain.

I check my phone, and awaiting me is an endless string of emails from friends and family who were in attendance at, or who heard about, last night's doings. Patty kindly offers to respond to them on my behalf. There's also a string of voice-mails, which I access.

One is from North Coast Theater management, deeply lamenting the loss of Andrew and Freddie and noting that, given the ongoing investigation, performances for this week have been canceled. A meeting between management and the cast and crew has been scheduled for 3 p.m. today in the downtown rehearsal hall to discuss the future of the production. Human Resources will be there as well. And Actors' Equity members will be hearing from their union rep.

Another voicemail is from my boss at the *Chronicle*, who requests that I give him a call. Which I do, once I grab a mug of black coffee.

Mark expresses genuine concern about my well-being and asks whether I have heard from poor Gwen, for he has not.

Then he gets down to what's really on his mind. "I'd like to put you on assignment and have you take the lead on the paper's coverage of the *Sweeney Todd* incident. Front page stuff."

I tell him that it is too soon for me to think about what happened with a clear head and too soon to turn last night's tragedy into copy. "And I've been asked to help out the detective in charge of the case, who needs to get her bearings around the theater, so there might be a conflict of interest."

"Got it. Perhaps you'd be willing to write a final behind-the-scenes piece—a reflection about last night—for the entertainment and arts section, when the time is right."

I'm about to tell him that I am not up for that either, but realize that interviewing my colleagues for this final article might uncover something that will help Detective Brandstätter with her investigation. I entered this enterprise as a clandestine critic, so I might as well live up to the title. I tell Mark that I'll write the piece.

While finishing my coffee, I leave a phone message for Gwen ("Hey. Just checking in to see how you are after such a horrific night. Call me. Call Mark."), a text for Larry's receptionist, as my friend requested ("Hi Tony. Let Larry know that I am readily available whenever he is."), and an email to members of the *Sweeney Todd* cast and crew ("By now, you've seen that we have a production meeting this afternoon. If anyone feels like talking about last night for a final article I'm writing about our show, or just feels like talking, let me know, and we can chat after the meeting.").

After some breakfast, I return to the theater so I can serve at the pleasure of Detective Brandstätter. There's a light dusting of snow on the roads, which has Clevelanders driving as if they've forgotten last winter and every winter before it, and I don't arrive downtown until 10:30 a.m.

At the theater stage door, I find an officer who is required to approve my entrance before letting me in. And there's another officer to take me through the backstage area to the stage. On the way there, I notice that the costumer is taking this opportunity to clean and mend everything in hampers and on hangers, and maintenance is being performed on a row of lights that have been lowered from the proscenium. There are a handful of crew members scurrying around, as well, who have no doubt been given permission to reset props and set pieces and get the stage ready for the re-start of Act I, whenever that will be, if at all.

The stage is still pretty much how I left it last night, except for some remnant yellow crime scene tape and the removal of the trail of blood and Andrew's dead body with arms and legs akimbo. Detective Brandstätter is on the stage, snooping around. She is in a different-style pantsuit than the one last night, but it's still gray, and just as capable of securely containing her brawn. It is a true testament to textiles.

"My forensics team is done with the scene," she yells to me. "Feel free to touch things."

"Do I have to?"

The detective asks if I came up with anything regarding the seven actors she identified as possible suspects. I walk over to her and return the playbill. "Well, you'll want to call a bartender and an oncologist," I reply, "but as far as I can see, there are perhaps three people who had the opportunity to murder Andrew during 'Johanna'."

I tell her that the obvious one is the unlikable outsider Jake Barnes, who plays Sweeney Todd and managed to have his hand on a real razor, rather than a prop. There's Brandon Steele, who plays Jonas Fogg. He's a bit of a bully, and may very well be a disgruntled cast member whose status with the company has been recently diminished. Chris O'Connell, who plays the romantic lead Anthony, is also a possibility. He is an itinerant actor and a musical theater gypsy who has made some unfortunate career choices. Maybe he made one more.

She processes what I have to say and, as a courtesy, shares with me that her forensics team discovered a syringe on the floor where my friend Freddie was found, along with a swollen puncture wound on his hand. Ganz had a similar wound.

"Our lab says it's propofol. Vets use it in small doses to drop an animal's blood pressure and slow its breathing before euthanasia. It makes them drowsy. It appears as if Ganz was given a small dose before his murder. In larger doses, it's what killed Michael Jackson. And Muñoz. I'm convinced that Muñoz was killed just to get him out of the way so Ganz could take his place in the barber chair."

"Why do you think that, if you don't mind me asking?"

"If the murderer just wanted Ganz dead, he or she could have just as easily killed him with the drug as dazed him. But the goal was to get him in the chair so he could be executed. As Larry suggested last night, whoever murdered Ganz intentionally did it in full view, on opening night, in Cleveland, to make a very public statement. I want to figure out what that statement is."

And then the detective shifts gears.

"There's something I need to understand. There was a twenty-five-minute intermission last night. Your stage manager told me this was typical on a sold-out opening night because of the long lines at the bar and in the bathrooms. That's twenty-five minutes for whoever killed Muñoz and Ganz to put things in motion. What was happening backstage during intermission?"

"As actors came off stage, some headed to the greenroom to eat, hydrate, check their phone for messages, and share thoughts about the first act. Others went directly to the backstage dressing rooms to change costumes for the 'God, That's

Good!' number. I went to the dressing room I share with two other ensemble players, grabbed my costume for the 'Johanna' number—just a hat, a coat, and a different pair of shoes—and hung it in the temporary changing booth in the wing. Then I headed for the greenroom. Nothing really out of the ordinary to report."

I then tell her that when we got the five-minute call from the stage manager—when she told us we had five minutes until the start of Act II—there was a mass exodus to the stage.

"She does the announcement, the call, in person?"

"She does this over the sound system from her booth on the mezzanine level at the rear of the theater. She lives there during the run of the show. The crew calls it 'the cage.'"

"Last night," says the detective, "your director told me that he and his wife were in the audience sitting with Ganz during the first act of the musical. When they got up to stretch and glad-hand during intermission, Ganz stayed in his seat, checking his phone. When they returned just before Act II started, he was gone. Did you see him backstage during the intermission?"

"No."

"No one we spoke to did, either. It is likely that Ganz was summoned backstage at the end of intermission and just before Act II began, so leaving his seat was not conspicuous and his appearance backstage was not seen because everyone was busy getting ready for the next act. His phone was missing when we checked the body, which suggests he was called or texted by the person who would kill him—someone he likely knows or is connected with this production, or he wouldn't have responded—and who probably took his phone."

I'm not sure if the detective is just thinking out loud or expects me to respond. I'm guessing the former, and wait for her to continue, which she does.

"Arrangements were most likely made to meet somewhere backstage that was unpopulated or dark."

Again, I'm not sure if I'm expected to chime in, but I think about backstage during the performance and say, "There are a lot of places they could have met, since all of backstage is unpopulated because of all that is going on to set up and perform 'God, That's Good!' And all of backstage is dark, lit only with some blue lights that make it possible to see what's in front of your face, but not much more."

"Since Ganz was injected with the same syringe as Muñoz, he was most likely summoned to the temporary changing booth where Muñoz was given the lethal injection," she says. "The murderer was waiting for him."

This cavalier way of discussing Freddie and Andrew getting killed is business as usual for Detective Brandstätter, but it's too much and too early in the morning for me. Plus, I was in the next changing booth when this all happened. My head spins a bit, and my heart suddenly gets heavy. The detective sees this in my face and, in that tender way of hers, ignores it and moves forward.

"When Act II begins," she continues, "the barbershop on the second floor is in darkness while 'God, That's Good!' is being performed. Is that correct?"

"Well, it's dark when I get up there toward the end of the musical number. But it is not totally black, since what is lighting the stage spills over and puts the barbershop in a sort of twilight. The stage and the barbershop are in total darkness between when 'God, That's Good!' ends and the 'Johanna' number begins, while there's applause."

"That's about thirty seconds of darkness," says the detective. Checking her notes, she adds, "When 'Johanna' begins, the character Anthony is on stage and lit only in spotlight. He sings for thirty seconds before the lights come up on the barbershop and the audience sees Sweeney with razor in hand and the first customer in the chair, and the song continues."

"That sounds right."

"Before that, you and Muñoz leave the stage during 'God, That's Good!' with about three minutes left in the number."

"Yup."

"That leaves those three minutes, plus the thirty seconds of applause between numbers, plus the first thirty seconds of 'Johanna' for Muñoz to be drugged and killed and Ganz to be drugged, dragged, and placed in the barber chair. That's four minutes, total. Four minutes is tight, but doable for someone who has given this some thought, mapped out the steps, and knows this musical inside and out."

Chapter 21

A Tenor in a
Non-Dancing Role

A FTER ESTABLISHING A timeline for the murders—approximately four minutes from Freddie's death in the changing booth to Andrew's in the barbershop—Detective Brandstätter starts walking across the stage to the ramp that leads to the crime scene.

"You were up on this platform, just offstage of the barbershop when Ganz was brought into the barbershop and murdered. Show me where you were."

While she follows me up the ramp, she asks, "You said it was dark but 'twilight' when you got to this platform. Could you see across the barbershop to the other platform about ten to twelve feet away?"

"No."

"Could you see if someone was already placed in the barber chair by the time you got to the platform?"

"I was preoccupied with frantically thinking through the next scene, and I have no reason to look into the barbershop, since there's nothing in there that I'm responsible for. So, no."

"Could you hear anything?"

"Only the sound of the amplified singing from below during what remained of 'God, That's Good!' and the sound of applause afterward. And then 'Johanna' kicks in and Anthony sings."

"Did anyone cross your path on the platform, going into or out of the barbershop, during your time there in the darkness?"

"Only Jake Barnes, the actor playing Sweeney. After he returns to the barbershop after interacting with Mrs. Lovett during 'God, That's Good!', he climbs up the ramp and goes into the barbershop for the beginning of the 'Johanna' number. He does this in the darkness, just as Anthony starts singing."

"He does this every time?"

"Every time. This is how it's been rehearsed, and this is how it's performed."

"Is he holding his razor?"

"It's always waiting for him in the barbershop. He walks over to the small table in the back to get it at the start of the musical number."

Detective Brandstätter pauses for a moment to think. "Between interacting with Mrs. Lovett during 'God, That's Good!' and crossing your path to get into the barbershop at the beginning of 'Johanna,' Jake Barnes doesn't really have the time to commit murder. And certainly not two murders. So unless he had help, Jake Barnes doesn't seem like a very viable suspect."

"I suppose not."

"If I'm the murderer and familiar with the staging of this show," continues the detective, "I'd bring Ganz into the barbershop from the offstage platform during the thirty seconds of total blackness during the applause between musical numbers. I wouldn't risk doing it in twilight. And I'd want to be out of the barbershop and heading down the ramp before Sweeney enters."

"And if the murderer is Chris O'Connell, the actor playing Anthony," I add, "he not only has just those thirty seconds of total blackness to bring in Andrew and head down the ramp, he has to go down the ramp, run all the way around the back of the set piece, and get into position on the stage to get lit and start singing 'Johanna'."

With that, the detective leads me across the barbershop and onto the other platform, where the murderer and a dazed Andrew recently stood. "Imagine I'm Ganz and you're Anthony. When I say 'go,'" she says, while taking out her phone and accessing its stopwatch function, "bring me to the barber chair, turn and run down the ramp, get yourself to where the spotlight hits Anthony, and start singing."

"Wait. What?"

"Go."

When I put my arm around Detective Brandstätter's waist, she allows herself to be a near-dead weight as we lurch to the chair. Walking those few steps to the center of the barbershop is hard work, and I imagine that dragging Andrew's long, semiconscious body was the same ("That's twelve seconds," I hear her say.). As instructed, I turn and bolt back to the platform, run down the ramp as my hamstrings tighten ("That's twenty seconds."), speed-walk around the length of the set with a muscle cramp building in my side, and hit the spot on stage where Anthony stands to sing his solo.

"Where's the singing?" she shouts, while glancing at the stopwatch on her phone and shaking her head. There's a brief silence until I am finally able to sing-speak—while bent over, gasping for breath, and trying not to vomit—a barely audible "I feel you, Johanna."

"Well," she says, while stopping the timer, "that wasn't impressive. Forty-five seconds."

Looking around backstage, she orders the younger, fitter

uniformed officer who had escorted me into the theater to come up to the platform to replicate our Anthony-as-the-murder's escape from the barbershop. "You have thirty seconds," she tells him.

In full sprint with long strides, it takes him thirty-seven seconds to hit his mark on the stage and, when he sings, "I feel you, Johanna," he is slightly pitchy, very red-faced, and panting like a poodle.

"Was the actor who plays Anthony, Chris O'Connell, panting last night?" asks the detective while looking down at me and the exhausted officer.

I try to put together a sentence, but, still sucking wind, all I can muster is: "Nope."

"Is he in as good of shape as this officer?"

I want to tell her that he recently spent a year-and-a-half stuffing himself with Disney cruise cuisine, but I'm still bent over with my hands on my hips. "He's a tenor . . . in a non-dancing role," is the best I can do.

"What does that mean?"

"Not in as good shape," I yell, expending all the air that was left in my lungs and feeling as if it will never be replaced. I have to sit down.

"Well, O'Connell is not likely our killer. Brandon Steele has just moved up in the ranks, unless there is someone else we have yet to consider," she says.

My phone rings.

It's Larry.

Chapter 22

I Am in the Dark Beside You

"Sandbag night fuse 200 to 214."

"Huh?"

"That's what Christine and I remember hearing during the show last night not long after intermission," says Larry over the phone. "Well, it's as close as we could agree on. The two comp seats you gave me were way to the left side of the house, near the farthest aisle that goes from the back entrance of the theater to the door that leads backstage. The emergency exit that Detective Brandstätter and I came through once all the cast and crew were gathered opens to that aisle. It was dark during the show, so we didn't see who was talking."

"You heard someone talking during the show?"

"And we thought it was pretty rude at the time." I can hear paper being unrumpled on the other end of the phone. "So, like I said, *Sandbag night fuse 200 to 214*, and then we heard *Sandbag night fuse 200 stop, trade up one toady, and I love it. Go.*"

I ask Larry to repeat all this so I can write it down and, as I do, I say, "This makes no sense."

"I know, right?" agrees Larry. "But that's what we heard. It sounded like someone was talking on the other end of a phone, like whoever was listening had them on speaker phone. It could have been an usher listening to something over a walkie talkie. Hard to tell."

"Was the voice male or female?" I ask, knowing that Detective Brandstätter would be asking me the same question after saying that these words make no sense.

"We both agreed it sounded female. Oh, and we heard the same voice again a little later, just after the applause for the meat pie number when Anthony starts singing 'Johanna.' We heard something like: *Sandbag right fuse 221, stop on a pony. And go.*"

I write that down as well. "Thanks, I guess. I'll share this with the detective."

"Got a nickname yet?"

"Working on it."

"Hey," says Larry before hanging up. "I spoke to your colleague Gwen this morning. I called her to see how she was holding up. She was a real mess last night. She said she was still pretty dazed, and I recommended that she see a trauma therapist, but she said her golden retriever would be all the therapy she would need. Plus, she's going to stay home from the paper and her classes for a few days. There are no extracurriculars she's missing—her fencing and debate seasons haven't started yet—and she said she's caught up with work at the paper. You should give her a call."

When I share the overheard gibberish with the detective and hand over the notebook where I wrote it, she asks an officer to find the house manager or head usher or get one of them on the phone if they aren't in the building. Within minutes, the house manager—a very round fellow in a Charlie Brown sweater vest and with a Lucy van Pelt attitude—trots down the theater's middle aisle toward Detective Brandstätter, who is now standing center stage. It is clear from how his steps slow the closer he gets to the stage that her size frightens the hell out of him. Welcome to the club.

"Last night," says the detective without introduction, "some patrons sitting by that far aisle overheard talking. They said it sounded like the person was on a phone. It was during the second act of the show. They heard the talking twice, a few minutes apart. Are there ushers stationed nearby?"

"There are quite a few ushers there after intermission to help people get back to their seats, but then only one patrols the area during the performance in case there's a need."

"A need?"

"A medical emergency. Someone wanting assistance. A disturbance."

"Did any usher report a disturbance, like someone talking on a phone during the show?"

"No, they didn't. There were no reports at all last night until, well, you know, Andrew Ganz. And if someone was talking on a phone, it would not happen twice. Ushers are instructed to take phones away from patrons who talk or text or take photos during a performance. It says so in the playbill and in the preshow announcement made by, you know, Andrew Ganz, and we take that very seriously."

"Does the usher patrolling the aisle have a walkie talkie?"

"He does not. Using them during a show would be disturbing to our patrons. If there's a problem, an usher handles it or reports to a designated head usher in the very back of the theater, who uses a phone on the wall that connects directly to my office."

"Thanks," says the detective.

"You might want to know that one of our ushers was absent and unaccounted for when the team met before being discharged last night. We gathered so I could tell them what a good job they did, and Ernie—the fellow who found the dead actor backstage—wasn't there and hadn't signed out. He's been with patron services for a while, and knows better."

As the house manager quickly turns and retreats, Detective Brandstätter calls out: "Thanks for your kind assistance," as if she were begrudgingly following some directive from a recent memo issued by her office's public relations officer. "What?!" she says to me when she sees the smirk on my face. "We all got a memo from the public relations officer."

The detective once again takes a look at the notebook. "*Sandbag night fuse 200 to 214,*" she reads aloud. "*Sandbag night fuse 200 stop trade up one toady and I love it. Go.* What does that mean?"

"No idea," I admit.

"That's stage direction," says a college-age crew member walking by and pushing a long wooden handle with a double-wide broom at the end. Her eyes are red, as if she'd been crying, which I imagine is a common reaction among the cast and crew to what had happened during last night's production.

"I'm sorry, what?" asks the detective.

"The words aren't right, but they sound just like stage management language. They're cues."

"Your name?"

"I'm Jennifer. You should be speaking to Jasmine, who is the stage right ASM. Hey, Jasmine!"

As Jasmine approaches, I lean toward Detective Brandstätter and stage whisper, "'ASM' means assistant stage manager," so that Jasmine can know from the get-go that the detective is absolutely clueless when it comes to anything theater related.

"I'm Detective Brandstätter. You might know Asher Kaufman from the show. Would you read what's written in his notebook? We think its stage direction, but the language is wrong. Can you make sense of this?"

The ASM, also red-eyed and not much older than Jennifer, seems none too pleased to be kept from the work she has ahead of her. She puts the armful of meat pie props that she was returning backstage on a nearby table and takes the pad from the detective. As she reads to herself, I apologize for my lousy handwriting.

"*Sandbag night fuse 200 to 214*. That sounds like *standby light cues 200 to 214*," says Jasmine, without hesitation. "That's a call to get ready for fourteen lighting cues."

Detective Brandstätter and I just stare, a bit stunned by how nonsense makes perfect sense in the right hands.

"*Sandbag night fuse 200 stop trade up one toady and I love it, go.* is weird, but it sounds familiar. It could be *stand by, light cue 200, spotlight fade up on Toby and Lovett*. And the *go* is the cue to hit the spotlights. Close enough, anyway."

More staring.

"How do you know this?" asks the detective, which is meant to be inquisitive, but, like so much of what she says, comes across as accusatory.

"It's my job to know this show backward and forward," says Jasmine, who—after being barked at by Kate, the stage manager, during weeks of rehearsals—is impervious to the detective's tone.

"Where in the show do light cues 200 to 214 happen?" I ask, knowing that the detective is unaware of the inner workings of a production.

"There are, let's see, two scenes in the show that feature Toby and Mrs. Lovett. Both are in Act II, and both require that they be hit with spotlights. But since we are talking light cues in the early 200s, it would not be during the song 'Not While I'm Around,' which happens much later in the show. These cues are from 'God, That's Good!' just after intermission."

"And," asks a rather nonplussed detective, "how about this one?" She points to the notepad, and Jasmine reads aloud, "*Sandbag right fuse 221 stop on a pony. And go.*"

After a moment's thought, she says, "Light cue 221 is a bit

later in the show, but not much. What's being called is *Stand by light cue 221, spotlight on Anthony. And go.*"

"And where in the show does this happen?" asks the detective.

"The start of 'Johanna,' when the spotlight operator stands by and, on 'go,' hits Anthony with light as he sings."

"Who hears all these light cues?" asks the detective.

"The person operating the lighting board, the guys on the spotlights, and both ASMs, me on stage right and Jamal on stage left. We're all on headsets."

"And who," asks the detective, "calls these lighting cues?"

"Kate, the stage manager," Jasmine and I say at the same time.

Chapter 23

Sandbag Right Fuse
221 Stop on a Pony

I KNOW I WAS brought in as just a theater liaison, and should speak when spoken to, but neither my critic's instincts, nor my mouth have turn-off switches.

"So, someone walking down the aisle to the door that leads backstage was listening for lighting cues on a headset?" I ask the detective. "Was that the murderer?"

Detective Brandstätter interrupts me by thanking Jasmine, the ASM, for her kind assistance and asking her to find Jamal and report to the officer stationed by the backstage door. "He'll have a few questions about your whereabouts during 'God, That's Good!' and the 'Johanna' reprise, and if you saw or heard anything out of the ordinary."

When Jasmine leaves, I pick up where I left off. "Was the killer trying to time the murder to what was happening on stage by listening to the stage manager on a headset?"

The detective is hesitant to comment on an ongoing investigation, but she realizes that I have skin in the game, both as a consultant and a cast member, and that we are off the record since I am no longer operating as a journalist.

"That's one possibility. Another is that Kate, the stage manager, could be an accomplice by adjusting the timing of the lighting cues to help the murderer avoid getting caught by staying in the dark. I'd ask her, but she did not come in this morning, even though her crew has. That's odd, right?"

"That's odd."

"I'm going to join the officer by the backstage door and ask the ASMs whether any of the lighting cues were changed or were late or early last night. Kate might very well be involved. You've been a great help, Asher, and I don't want to take up any more of your time. I know you'll keep everything we've discussed confidential. Thanks for your kind assistance."

As the detective turns to leave, I suggest that she might want to ask the ASMs to take a look inside the stage manager's booth. "I know your forensics team went through it, but there could be something in there that your team didn't know was significant in the running of a theatrical production."

She stops, stares at me for a beat, and says, "Maybe I'm not done with you yet. Would you mind meeting the ASMs at the booth and report anything they find? I don't speak their language." She reaches into her coat pocket, detaches a key from a ring, tosses me the key to the booth, and continues her walk to the backstage door.

After waiting outside the cage for about fifteen minutes, Jasmine and Jamal show up, and we pop our heads into the small space. There's not much there except a swivel chair, a metal console with assorted levels and dials, two music stands, and two monitors.

I see that Kate left her script on one of the music stands, and ask Jasmine about that.

"The script always stays in the booth so an ASM can run the show in case there's a problem and the stage manager can't make a performance, which rarely, if ever, happens. The score stays, as well, which is on the other music stand."

Jamal can see that I am about to ask why the stage manager has a score, and says, "There's so much music in this show that Kate wrote the cues she calls in the score and uses that during most of the production. I worked a production of *Les Misérables,* and she did the same."

"About eighty-five percent of *Sweeney* is sung or under-scored," adds Jasmine at the moment Jamal finishes his sentence, as if the two were twins connected at the brain stem.

They are more than eager to talk about their craft, and I would imagine that few are actually interested in hearing about it. But I ask about the two monitors on the console.

"One has a feed to the orchestra pit so that Kate can watch the conductor and time lighting, sound, and deck cues with the music," says Jasmine.

"Those are cues for things that happen on stage, like set rotations, moving tables and chairs, or bringing on and taking off props," says Jamal. "The second monitor shows a stage feed. This gives Kate a closer look at what's happening on stage than she can see from the booth. When the stage goes to black, there's a cool infrared setting so that the stage—"

"Hey, there's something weird," interrupts Jasmine.

But before I can ask what, the sight and sound of crew members walking up the aisles and heading toward the lobby exit reminds us of the 3 p.m. production meeting that's been called by North Coast Theater management. I lock up the booth and the three of us hustle out of the Hedley Theatre and head toward the rehearsal studio down the street. Further dissection of the cage will have to wait.

Chapter 24

Another Opening

WE SEEM TO be the last to arrive. There's coffee, a side table full of bite-sized snacks, and enough chairs around a large round table for North Coast Theater's managing director, our director and musical director, a representative from human resources, the cast, and the crew.

As everyone takes a seat, I take a quick attendance and see that neither our stage manager nor our Sweeney Todd are here.

The managing director offers his greetings, asks that we turn off our cell phones, leads a contemplative moment of silence for Andrew and Freddie, and starts delving into the business at hand—the future of our production in light of last night's tragedy and our leading man being behind bars.

While he does, I do my clandestine critic and inept detective thing by spying on everyone in the room. This is a rare opportunity to see whether personal dynamics, body language, and who is talking with whom informs or adds to Detective Brandstätter's list of viable suspects. Of course, I have no idea what I'm looking for, but the managing director is a terribly slow-talking, droning public speaker, and I'm happy to occupy myself with other things.

I watch the crew for a while, who are all seated together

and rigorously writing down in their iPads everything being said. They do so with freakish though admirable synchrony. Nothing out of the ordinary here.

From the distinct odor of ethanol coming from one end of the table, I see Tony Silver, our Signor Adolfo Pirelli, who seems to have already fallen asleep during the brief, mid-day presentation. Nothing out of the ordinary here, either.

I notice that Erin Andrews is not sitting next to her spouse, Sylvia, which I find curious until I see that Erin, who plays Johanna, is sitting next to Chris O'Connell, her *Sweeney* character's counterpart, Anthony. Sylvia is sitting next to the young man who plays Tobias, the young assistant to her Mrs. Lovett. It makes perfect sense in a production meeting like this that actors are paired based on their characters and not their preferences, which is why untethered ensemble members like me are pretty much scattered around the table.

My eyes shift to Brandon Steele, who seems as though he would rather be anywhere else and prefers being seated between two empty chairs rather than his on-stage partners. Before I can move on to the next actor at the table, my attention is immediately drawn to the far side of the rehearsal studio and my gut reaction to it is a slow and all too audible, "What the fuck?!"

There I see a handcuffed and menacing Jake Barnes, standing in his Gothic Sweeney costume and pale makeup. This is startling, and the room turns silent as others, prompted by my unfortunate exclamation, see him as well.

"Oh, and our Sweeney has been just released from custody," announces the managing director with a huge smile.

Jake slowly removes the fake cuffs, waves them about as if doing a striptease, and starts singing a rousing version of the lyrics from the opening number of our musical, which ask that we attend the tale of Sweeney Todd. Everyone in the room, except for the clueless human resources representative, joins in as Jake shakes hands, pats backs, and musses hair before taking his seat at the table.

"All charges have been dropped," he shouts, and it is announced that after taking the rest of the weekend off to heal, we have been given permission to have some fresh-up rehearsals this week, reopen our production next Friday night, and extend the run by a week. When the details about scheduling, security, and payment have been laid out, the meeting is adjourned.

As people start to leave, several actors come by to tell me that they would be happy to talk with me about last night for my article, that it would be cleansing. We set up a day and time for a phone call or schedule to talk during a break at a rehearsal.

Jake grabs me from behind and gives me a long, hard hug. "Hey, there's no hard feelings about you thoroughly tackling me on stage," he says with what comes awfully close to earnestness. "Great hit, by the way."

"And no hard feelings about you almost killing me," I reply.

I ask about his release from jail, and he says that the crew is responsible. "When I wasn't onstage during 'God, That's Good!' I was in the wings, flirting like I do. The crew vouched for my whereabouts. Excuse me while I go hug them too."

Before he leaves, I tell him about this final behind-the-scenes piece I'm writing and how it focuses on what took place on opening night. I ask him about his experience on stage and if he had any sense that a real razor had replaced the prop.

"You know," he says while thinking hard, as if it hurts, "the whole scene felt off to me. The razor felt different in my hand—I remember thinking that it was heavier and sturdier, colder too—and the guy in the chair seemed larger and less Hispanic than before. But what can you do when you are in the middle of a big song in the middle of a big show? I thought the blood looked different, as well."

"And then there I was in that chair, with that heavier, sturdier, colder, bloody razor at my neck." I point to the small bandage below my ear.

"Crazy, right?!" he says with astounding lack of awareness.

I suppose that it takes great dedication to your art to plug through a song despite a decapitation. But his casually moving on to the next decapitation does not leave me feeling the love. So I ask him about his name change. For the article.

"What made you go with Jake Barnes?"

"It was recommended by my agent," he says. "A real smart guy who thought it would work well for me professionally. He's my ex-agent and ex-friend, actually, because he was sleeping with my wife. Because I was sleeping with his."

"Did you know that you now share the name of an Ernest Hemingway character who is impotent?" He did not.

"Did you know that your ex-agent has quite the sense of humor?" He did not.

"Crazy, right?!" I say with a smile.

As I head back to the theater after the meeting, I check my phone messages and see that there's one from Kate, the *Sweeney* stage manager. "Hi Asher," she says. "I've been so disturbed by what happened to Andrew and Freddie last night that I've pretty much fallen off the radar. I won't be at today's meeting, but would love to take you up on your invitation to be interviewed for your final article. There's so much to talk about. How about you come to my apartment tomorrow for lunch at noon?" She leaves me her address, and I text that I'll be there.

Chapter 25

As You Like It

FROM THE EDITOR: This is the fourth in a series of behind-the-scenes articles by critic Asher Kaufman about his adventures in North Coast Theater's production of *Sweeney Todd*. The show is ending its run in Taos, New Mexico, and opens in Cleveland in one week.

There was an understanding between the stage manager Kate and me throughout rehearsals for *As You Like It*, well before *Sweeney Todd*. She never talked with me directly and we never had eye contact, and I was too intimidated to ever ask why.

But after the opening night performance of the show, when I returned to my dressing room to change into my street clothes, she left on the makeup table a clipping of an old review I had written.

Kate and I were among the last ones to leave the theater that night, and I yelled ahead to her as we both walked down the now-dark and empty backstage hallway toward the theater's rear exit. I was off to meet friends and family at a nearby restaurant for an after-show celebration and post-mortem. And her plans, I imagined, were to disappear all alone into the artificial light of the outdoor parking lot, get into a battered car littered with old scripts, fast-food wrappers, and heartbreak, and head back to a tiny house that was empty save for a dozen cats that ignored her the way that she ignored me. I was just guessing, of course, since I knew nothing about her whatsoever.

"What's with the newspaper clipping?"

She stops, turns, and speaks to me for the first time since the first day of rehearsal. "That's from a North Coast show I stage managed years ago. It was my debut in the cage, and it was the only time my name ever appeared in a review. No one notices stage management," she said, "and it meant a lot to me."

"So why did you leave it on my table instead of coming by to chat?" I asked. "And why haven't we ever chatted? I thought you hated me."

She went on to explain that she didn't want to get emotional in front of a cast member because she had a well-earned reputation for being a hard-ass and didn't want to screw that up.

So . . . Kate has feelings.

I invited her to join me and my friends, but she jokingly said that the official Stage Management Handbook, which does not exist, forbids social interaction with non-union actors in very small roles.

So . . . Kate has a sense of humor.

After we exited the theater, she went her way and I went mine, and she has ignored me ever since.

So . . . Kate is consistent. Stage managers!

Chapter 26

Warn the Children

ON THE WALK back to the theater from the meeting with North Coast Theater management, I catch up to Jasmine and Jamal to ask them what they found in the stage management booth that was so interesting.

Jasmine says it was the headphones on the back of Kate's chair. "ASMs wear a wireless headset during a performance so we can move around backstage and control our territory."

"Actually," adds Jamal, "everyone in charge of some aspect of the show's technical production wears wireless. But Kate wears a set that plugs into her board in the cage, so she can be patched into and switch between the conductor, the light operators, and each of us if she needs to tell us something specific."

I shake my head and say, "I'm not sure what you're getting at."

"This set of headphones on Kate's chair, the pair she used last night, is wireless," says Jamal, while Jasmine nods in agreement. "That was unexpected."

When I walk into the theater lobby, I find Detective Brandstätter talking to some officers and wait my turn. When I tell her that I have a few things to share, we walk into the house and she points to a row of seats, which is her shorthand for "Please, Asher, have a seat so we can take a moment or two to converse as normal people do."

I tell her about what the ASMs discovered in the stage manager's booth and find that she knows about the headphones from the forensics report. What she did not know is that Kate does not typically wear wireless or that they are not what she needs to best run a show.

I also tell her that Jake Barnes has been released from jail and, of course, she knows this as well. What she did not know is the literary source of Jake's pseudonym, which has nothing at all to do with the case but makes her smile and shake her head in disbelief.

As if guided by the rules of self-disclosure—the sense of obligation to reveal something personal after someone has done the same—the detective starts sharing with me what she has discovered about this case so far. Of course, it is more likely that she is just using me as a sounding board as she goes through her checklist of accumulated facts and findings. I'm good either way.

"The stage door in the rear of the backstage area is always well secured during performances, and there were no unauthorized entrances or exits made on opening night," she tells me. "The same goes from the front doors to the theater lobby. The killer was still in the building at the time I arrived."

She adds, "There were dozens of deliveries of flowers and gifts for the cast at the stage door before the show began, which were handed to the security guard, logged, and handed over to crew members to bring to the greenroom. The guard at the post is who he says he is, and is not a suspect."

There is nothing linking anyone in the North Coast Theater administration to the murders. They've been cleared.

The crew's whereabouts during the production have been confirmed by multiple sources, and there is nothing suspicious. They've been cleared as well.

The twelve members of the orchestra and the conductor

did not leave the pit for the entirety of the show and don't have direct access to the stage during the performance. The detective marveled at how their highly disciplined bladders are like those of police officers on a late-night stakeout. When I inform her that the orchestra has its own greenroom and restroom under the stage, she admits that officers "are very resourceful with an empty soda can."

"The missing ninety-two-year-old usher who found Muñoz is a person of interest, but not a suspect," she says. There is more concern that he might have been disposed of if he had happened to see the murderer in action. "My people are looking into that," she adds.

There were no fingerprints on the syringe found in the changing booth where Freddie was killed, suggesting that the murderer wore gloves. The only fingerprints found on Sweeney's razor were those of the actor playing Sweeney, suggesting that whoever planted it had worn gloves.

"I talked with Jasmine and Jamal," says the detective. "Both noted that multiple light cues were either late or early during 'God, That's Good!' and 'Johanna' on opening night. Nothing disruptive, but this was an unusual occurrence, they said, since the stage manager is a perfectionist who has, in their words, 'ridden our asses for far lesser mistakes.' And now, with what you have said about the wireless headphone, there will most certainly be a second interview with Kate."

The detective stands and says, "I'm about to check out local bars to see if any bartenders can confirm Tony Silver's alibi of wetting his whistle during the time of the murder, starting with the place across the street. They make great burgers." And just like that, although a tad awkwardly, the detective asks if I want to join her for dinner, her treat for all the assistance I've offered.

I thank her, but tell the detective that I am expected

home for dinner. "Nothing fancy. It's Pasta Saturday at the Kaufmans'. There'll be plenty of food, so how about you join us at about 6:30 p.m.? Patty and the kids would love to meet you."

"That sounds good," she says, and means it. I give her the address—although she probably has an extensive file on me, including my address—and take off. On my way home, I phone Patty to tell her that we will have a guest tonight and to warn the children.

Chapter 27

Goldberg in a Pantsuit

WHEN I GET home, I find both kids at the kitchen table doing homework and eager for an excuse not to. I sit down to bring them up to speed on what my life has been like these last two days, but discover that Patty had already told them about *Sweeney Todd*, though with greater delicacy and selectivity than I would have managed.

It is clear that what they really want to talk about is Detective Brandstätter.

Austin quickly outgrew an early fascination with professional wrestling, but had amassed an impressive collection of WrestleMania memorabilia that still resides on the floor of his closet. I ask him to go bring back his Goldberg action figure—a twelve-inch, posable plastic version of the bald and brawny pay-per-view gladiator. Goldberg was a World Championship Wrestling Triple Crown winner whose most famous move was refusing to wrestle on Yom Kippur. I ask Zoey to go pull her favorite Nancy Drew novel from her beloved 56-book collection of the American mystery stories about a teenage sleuth that she had inherited from Patty, who inherited them from her mother.

When they return, I place the hard-bodied Goldberg on the kitchen table next to the hardbound copy of the 1939 novel *The Clue of the Tapping Heels*. I ask the kids to imagine

that the musclebound, six-foot, four-inch, 285-pound Goldberg is female, has long black hair, and—just as Nancy Drew
wore pants while working a case—is donning a gray pantsuit
rather than a standard-issue spandex wrestler's leotard. She is
also endowed with Nancy Drew's intelligence, curiosity, and
survival instincts.

"That," I tell them, "is Detective Brandstätter. And she's
coming over for dinner tonight." Their eyes are the size of
saucers.

Chapter 28

I'll Be Back

THE DOORBELL RINGS. As Detective Brandstätter walks through the front door of my house and takes off her coat, I turn to introduce her to the family and see that my wife and two children are frozen where they stand.

"I get this all the time," says the detective as she hands off the coat and the bottle of red wine she picked up on the way over. She approaches Patty, thanks her for the invitation on such short notice, bends down and gives her a huge, prolonged hug. I can see that my wife's basic instincts are jostling between fight and flight, but she is locked in the detective's warm embrace and just gives into it. The result of the hug is immediate: Patty melts.

The detective moves on to my sixteen-year-old son, offers him her hand, and his pubescent man-paw disappears into her massive appendage for a handshake. "Ow," she says earnestly while shaking. And so he giggles, which is something I have not heard out of him since well before his voice changed.

Taking a step to the right, the detective takes my twelve-year-old daughter by the waist and gently, effortlessly, lifts her up so they are eye-to-eye. "You are adorable," she says before lowering a beaming Zoey for a gentle landing.

Who knew the detective had a soft spot?

The dinner is a delicious spaghetti Bolognese, my recipe,

which the detective inhales with such vivacity that you can almost hear the carbohydrates being torn from the pasta and turning into muscle mass with each bite. The wine, an Italian Barolo, is appropriate for the meal, quite expensive, and quickly drained. And the conversation is easy and an equal opportunity interaction.

Detective Brandstätter spends most of the meal inquiring about Patty and the kids and, to my surprise, her questioning doesn't come across like waterboarding. The kids ask all about her as well, and, among other things, I learn that her first name is Brigitte. She makes sure to tell my family how helpful I've been during the investigation, which I find remarkably gracious.

When she excuses herself to make a quick phone call to the office for updates and says, "I'll be back," I can tell by the way she looks back to see if the kids are smiling that she does this on purpose, always has, just to recognize the Terminator in the room and put people at ease. The kids are, of course, smiling and very much at ease.

As dinner draws to a close, the detective asks if we can talk some shop, and I suggest that we head into my office. Before we do, she insists on clearing the table, helping with the dishes, and chatting up Patty as if they were besties.

And so, in just one evening, Zoey has found herself her very own, larger-than-life Nancy Drew action figure with Kung Fu grip who, in years to come, will become a trusted confidante. She will even call on the detective to rescue her from a blind date turned abusive, knowing that the detective will be the one to firmly talk sense into the boy while I would have stood by, quaking with anger and bad intentions.

And, in just one evening, Austin became a card-carrying feminist—he was more than half-way there already—whose idea of female beauty underwent a paradigm shift. Visions of the detective will haunt his dreams until a girl more down-scaled, closer in age, and actually accessible enters his life.

And, in just one evening, Patty made a very good friend at whose hospital bedside she will sit, in lieu of long-estranged family members, when Detective Brandstätter is shot and mortally wounded while walking into a convenience store robbery to pick up some soy milk a few years from now.

Me? I've been given permission to call the detective Brigitte. Just not outside of the house or until this case has been solved.

Once the two of us settle in my office, the detective brings me up to speed on the missing-in-action usher, Ernie, whose absence after finding Freddie's body was suspicious.

"When I left the theater tonight, I stopped by the bar across the street to see if the bartender remembers seeing the drunk actor who plays Pirelli. That guy is certainly a creature of habit. The bartender remembered him arriving at around 9 p.m., in costume, which was before the murder. The place was pretty empty at that time of night, which was after the dinner crowd had left and well before the shows in Playhouse Square let out and the place fills up again."

She said that the bartender also recalled an old fellow in a red sports coat coming through the door not long after all the police cars arrived at the theater at around 10 p.m. "He said that the guy sat at the bar, cried about just having seen something terrible, and ordered shot after shot until he fell asleep. The bartender put him in a booth until he came to and then he put him in a cab. My office will follow up with both of them in the morning, but neither is a suspect."

Of the cast members, that leaves Brandon Steele. And the detective also tells me that she's been thinking about Kate. A lot. "When Larry overheard lighting cues coming from the headphones worn by a person in the aisle, I thought that it was the killer listening in on Kate to gather information. Or Kate could be an accomplice purposefully giving information that could assist in the murder. But headphones are made to keep other people from hearing what is being said over them."

"This is especially true in the theater when a production is going on," I add.

"Larry didn't so much overhear what was coming from the headphones as overhear what was being said by the person wearing them. And what was being said was a series of light cues on the fly, on the way down the aisle to the backstage to kill Muñoz and execute Ganz. Larry said the voice sounded female. That was Kate using wireless headphones. You're the theater guy. Can you come up with any reason why she had a wireless set last night that has nothing to do with committing a crime?"

"I can't. But I could ask her tomorrow when I'm at her house. We're getting together for lunch so I can interview her for a final behind-the-scenes article I'm writing for the paper."

"Oh, I don't think so. You can't go to her house."

"I can. I'll be a journalist working on a story. Freedom of the press."

"Well, you can't go by yourself. It's dangerous."

I quickly assess my options and know that I either don't go or we go together. "I'll meet you there around noon."

Chapter 29

42nd Street

ARRIVE AT KATE's low-rise apartment complex, which is in one of the funkier parts of the newly gentrified Tremont neighborhood on the west side of the city, at around 11:45 a.m. The sky is a beautiful blue, the air is chilly, and I am a nervous wreck. Between *As You Like It* and *Sweeney Todd,* I've been in the same room as Kate, but we never really talked and I know nothing at all about her. Now we're having lunch and she might be a killer. I am so not built for this.

As I drive around the building looking for a parking spot on the street, I notice an odd scattering of identical black four-door Fords with black-tinted windows parked in the rear and in the front. Their lack of distinction suggests, even to me, that they must be unmarked cop cars that are backing up Detective Brandstätter. But they are so laughably conspicuous—especially in this artsy neighborhood—that I expect Jackie Chan with Chris Tucker to be sitting in one of them and Martin Lawrence with Will Smith to be sitting in the other.

I find a vacant spot in the front to park and see the detective exiting a third black four-door Ford to meet me by the building's entrance. ·

"Some things to know," she says, once again without the social niceties one expects when greeting someone you just invited for dinner and who has embraced your family as her own. "This is your interview, so take the lead. I'm here for the ride. But if things turn south, and they might, I'll step up. When I do, excuse yourself and get out of the apartment and out of the way."

"Good morning," I say with a nervous smile so wide that even Detective Brandstätter should be able to catch the sarcasm and the anxiety behind it. There are no visible signs that she has.

Kate's one-bedroom, one-bath apartment is on the second floor. She responds to the front door buzzer and lets us in. When the detective and I turn the corner at the top of the first flight of stairs, we find Kate standing on the landing by her opened apartment door and taken aback by the uninvited guest.

"I'm sorry that I had to bring Detective Brandstätter along. I've been helping out with the investigation—just teaching the detective about the ways of musical theater—and now she just follows me around like a puppy. I couldn't just leave her in the car."

Kate takes our coats, points the way into her apartment, and asks if she should bring in some lunch before we chat, all the while with her eyes fixed on Detective Brandstätter.

"Thanks, maybe later," I say as we head into the living room. Our host sits in a cushioned chair on the far side of a small coffee table in the middle of the room as I sit on the matching couch across from her. The detective has already planted herself in a straight-backed chair by the door, which is well behind me but directly in Kate's sight line.

"Thanks for letting me interview you for this article," I say as I take a small tape recorder out of my pocket and lay it between us on the table. "Originally, I was going to write a piece that summarized my experiences with *Sweeney Todd*, but now I'd really like for it to be a forum for everyone else's experience from last night."

"That's a great idea. It must have been so traumatic for everyone on the stage. I know it was terrifying for my crew and they would love to talk with you. I was in my booth at the back of the theater watching everything on my monitors. I couldn't believe what I was seeing."

I ask her how the production was proceeding up until "Johanna." I ask her if she had noticed anything peculiar leading up to the tragedy. I ask her about her quick reaction to Andrew's death and what she was thinking as she took charge of the situation.

She answers each question calmly but always with her eyes focused over my shoulder and locked in on the detective's unblinking, emotionless, intimidating stare.

The production was going smoothly, she says. There was nothing out of the ordinary. Taking charge is what a stage manager does.

"You wear a plug-in headset in your booth during a show, is that correct?" asks Detective Brandstätter from her chair. So much for her just being here for the ride.

"Yes."

The detective rises, walks toward the two of us, and sits with me on the couch. As she does, she reaches for my tape recorder, shuts it off, and places it aside. From her suit coat pocket, she takes her own small tape recorder and puts it on the table. "This is OK, right?"

Kate nods.

"But on opening night of *Sweeney Todd* you wore something different, a wireless headset."

"No. Yes," she says.

"Why?"

"My plug-in pair broke."

Silence.

"It didn't break, actually," she adds, but I couldn't get it to operate properly. It was a problem during tech rehearsals. So I swapped it for another pair. A wireless pair. It was the only pair I could find."

"I was told that some lighting cues got called early and some got called late, which would explain your faulty headset."

"That's true."

"Only that wasn't during tech rehearsals. It was during opening night with the wireless headset."

More silence.

"It took nearly the first act for me to adjust to the new set," says Kate.

"The miscues didn't happen until Act II. Just before Ganz's murder."

Kate's eyes shift toward me, and I can see a small tear forming on one of her eyelids, where it lingers and gains mass. And then, looking back at the detective as the tear slowly falls, she says, "I needed the wireless on opening night to still stage manage the show while I left the cage and went backstage to dispose of Freddie Muñoz and kill Andrew Ganz."

My jaw drops at the confession. Detective Brandstätter's stare doesn't falter and her cadence doesn't miss a beat as she reads Kate her Miranda Rights notification and continues the questioning.

"The theater's stage door log shows that, well before the show began on opening night, flowers were delivered for actors and someone delivered a small package wrapped as a gift for you. Can I assume that a straight-blade razor was in that package?"

"Yes, that's right. And a pair of disposable gloves."

"The package was not delivered by a delivery service," adds the detective. "You had help. Someone who was at the show that night?"

No answer. More slow-developing tears.

"You left the headset in your booth by accident or on purpose?"

"I was thrown off by Andrew nearly falling off the stage after tumbling down the chute instead of landing in the pile of mannequins. When that happened, it was my job to halt the production. That was not the plan. I had to leave the booth to take charge of what was happening on stage. When you let me go home after questioning me backstage, the police didn't allow me to return to the cage, saying that everything was in lockdown. I was surprised to see you here today," she tells the detective, "but I knew that someone would find the headset and raise questions. And those questions would lead to answers that would eventually lead to me."

"Why did you kill Muñoz?"

"I didn't mean to. I used half of the drug in the syringe to incapacitate Freddie and the other half to incapacitate Andrew, but I didn't account for Freddie being so skinny or allergic or whatever killed him. I didn't have time to tech this through. I didn't learn that he had died until the next day. I felt terrible. I just wanted Freddie out of the way so that Andrew could be killed in the barber chair."

"Why was it important that Ganz be killed on stage?"

"Asher knows."

The detective's intimidating stare shifts my way, which finds me wide-eyed and rapidly shaking my head from side to side, using the universal signal for astonished cluelessness.

"Can he and I talk," Kate asks, "for his article?"

"Sure," says the detective, "but you'll have to keep it short and do it in cuffs. And my recorder is on."

With that, Detective Brandstätter stands and Kate stands as well, turning around so the detective can apply the cuffs.

As she sits, Kate reminds me that during the opening night for *As You Like It* she had given me a copy of an old review I had written that mentioned her stage management debut. "I told you that this was the first time my name had been mentioned in a review. It was also the last. Stage management is never covered by critics."

"I remember that night."

She tells me that stage management was the last thing she ever wanted to do for a career in the theater. She had trained as an actor, "but Andrew Ganz made it clear that I wasn't good enough to get hired by North Coast Theater. I showed up for auditions so many times and came away empty that Andrew took me aside and suggested that I consider a career behind the scenes. He gave me permission to observe and then work with his stage crew. And he hired me for that first time in the chair. He said that I might pick up some things from the actors I work with and promised to set up an audition when he thought I was ready."

"It sounds like Andrew gave you a great gift," I say.

"The audition never happened. I just stage managed, and every time I did—sitting in the dark cage by myself, night after night, show after show—I'm far from the excitement that originally attracted me to the stage and, despite my hard work, I'm invisible. For years, during every production, I'm reminded that this is my life and Andrew is responsible."

"You killed Andrew Ganz for revenge?

"It's been on my mind for quite a while."

"Why kill Andrew during *Sweeney Todd* and not during *As You Like It*?" I ask.

"The script actually calls for a character to be standing center stage wielding a sharp object and putting it to the throat of another character."

I give a sideways glance to the detective and silently mouth, "Told you so."

"OK, Kate, one last question. Why kill Andrew on the

opening night in Cleveland, and not the opening night in Taos?"

Just a small smile crosses her face as she stands and gives the nod to the detective that she is done and ready to leave. As Kate turns to walk away, I offer my condolences for her pet.

"What's that?" she says while walking.

"I assumed you had a pet euthanized so you could access the propofol to use on Freddie and Andrew. That can't be easy to come by."

"Who in the world would do such a thing?!" she says with an incredulous look on her face. "I just sweet-talked a desperate vet tech I met on OkCupid."

The detective grabs her recorder, takes Kate's arm, and leads the way outside the building. I grab my recorder and the coats and walk behind them. As I do, I look around the apartment and see that the walls are covered with framed posters of famous musicals. I hadn't noticed this before because, well, I had been a bit preoccupied with sharing space with a potential killer and had the detective looking over my shoulder the whole time.

One of the posters is for *42nd Street*, with its classic depiction of a yellow-haired, starry-eyed chorus girl sitting inside a circle that is surrounded by red, as if she were the bullseye of a target—an unknown about to be hit with fame and fortune. Kate, it seems, is another actor with Broadway in the rear-view mirror. What happens to a dream deferred? It depends on whether you have a vendetta, a razor, and a syringe.

Chapter 30

Collateral Damage

WHEN WE GET outside, the detective hands Kate off to an officer who is waiting on the lawn and who walks her to one of the unmarked cars. Her final words before being lowered into the backseat are, "I made sandwiches. You'll have to help yourselves."

"Well, that was easy," I say to Detective Brandstätter as I hand over her coat.

"No doubt due to your shrewd interrogation skills. Euthanasia? Really?"

"Sarcasm, right? It doesn't look good on you."

"Getting a confession from inexperienced killers is not very hard. They either get so flustered by their inadequate lies or get so caught up in them that they just surrender as the easiest way out. Plus, Kate knew someone would find the headset and put the pieces together. She confessed because she got caught. And, thanks to you, she got what she wanted."

"What was that?"

"Notoriety. She hated being a stage manager, but what she hated more was being invisible while doing it. Your article will put stage management in the arts and entertainment section of the *Chronicle*. The murder will put it on the front page of every other paper."

Reflecting back on what just happened in Kate's apartment, I say, "She was obviously protecting someone who was also involved in the murders."

"Absolutely," says the detective, "but not an accomplice. The more I look at what went down, the more I realize that killing Ganz on stage was an opportunity for Kate, but not the ultimate goal."

"What does that even mean?"

She explains that the razor that killed Ganz and the gloves that covered Kate's prints when she placed the razor in the barbershop came to the theater in a package. But Kate had never said that the syringe and the propofol came that way. She had brought those in herself.

After a moment to gather her thoughts, put the pieces together, and give them a dry run in her head, the detective says, "I think the razor was to carry out someone else's plan for an onstage murder that required Kate's assistance and had nothing to do with Ganz. Kate was the accomplice for whoever sent or delivered the package. Maybe the razor's delivery was a signal, a green light, that the plan devised by someone else was moving forward and that Kate was to swap out the razors."

"And the propofol?"

"Kate's idea, to carry out her own plan to drug and kill Ganz while she was assisting in a different murder."

"What makes you think that?"

"Kate said she was thrown off by the way Ganz nearly fell off the stage after he was killed. She said she had to halt the production, which was 'not the plan.' *The* plan. Her plan was for no one to notice that Ganz had been killed, at least not yet, and for the play to continue so the other murder could take place. Tell me, Asher, what would have happened next in the play, after Sweeney's first customer was executed?"

As my mind runs through the show's timeline, thinking

about the scenes that follow from where the song "Johanna" begins, Detective Brandstätter reaches over, pulls at the corner of the bandage on my neck in one painful stroke, and answers her own question. "You were next in the chair. Do you have any enemies, Asher?"

"Wait. What? Freddie was supposed to be in the chair before me."

"Muñoz was injected in the changing booth just so Kate could get Ganz on stage and in the barber chair in his place. If the original plan had been carried out without Kate's innovation, Muñoz would have been killed with Sweeney's razor and fallen through the trapdoor into the pile of mannequins—just to move on to the real target. Either way," says the detective, "Muñoz was collateral damage in an effort to get to you."

"What? That's ridiculous."

The detective's expression tells me that it isn't.

"I can't imagine anyone wanting me dead. I'm just a critic. And I'm going home."

I start walking toward my car, but the detective asks me to hold up. "You were someone's target, Asher, and the architect of your attempted murder wasn't Kate. That's the person she's protecting, and that person is still out there. I want to make a phone call that will give you some protection, and then I'm going to escort you home. But first I want to go back inside the apartment and get a sandwich."

Chapter 31

Minoring in Pharmacology

THE CICADAS MUST be in season because Detective Brandstätter was kidding about the sandwich. But she was not kidding about the phone call. She arranges for an unmarked vehicle to park in front of my house overnight until she has an opportunity to further question Kate and perhaps discover who put her up to exchanging razors during *Sweeney Todd*.

I call Larry, tell him about the attempt on my life, and ask whether he can clear his professional calendar for the rest of the day and keep me company. The unmarked vehicle is fine, but I'd like Larry in the house with the family. He's absolutely harmless, but he's a giant-sized deterrent and a calming influence. He says that he will have to be on call but can meet me at my house within the hour.

The detective follows me home and stays by my side until Larry arrives, which I find overprotective and precious until I realize that she just wants to hang with Patty and the kids. Before she leaves with a Tupperware container filled with the leftover Bolognese, the three of us head to my office—away from Patty and the kids—to brainstorm about who would want me dead.

I have to interrupt Larry after ten minutes of listing everyone I might have somehow pissed off over the years and the detective stops writing down their names when she senses that he has another ten minutes in him.

"I think Brandon Steele would want me dead," I admit. "I've given Brandon some pretty bad reviews over the years. Deservingly so, but I think I've taken more pleasure than I should have at his expense. I once wrote that seeing him on stage was like 'a sobering interlude of minimum-security imprisonment.'"

"That was a good one," says Larry.

"When Brandon was in last year's production of *Clue: The Musical,* I called him 'the musical theater equivalent of Ambien.' That probably did not sit well."

Larry is working hard at taking me seriously, but Detective Brandstätter acknowledges that people have killed for less.

"The thing is," I continue, "Brandon now has the small role of Jonas Fogg in *Sweeney Todd*—a role that has the distinction of being the only character in the entire musical who does not sing or dance. He might be blaming me. This might be the straw that broke the camel's back. The match in the powder barrel. The end of the line."

"What with Kate's arrest and another killer on the loose," says the detective on her way out the door, "it would certainly be a justified safeguard to put a watch team on Steele. Stay home. I'll keep you posted, should anything develop."

The detective gives me a quick hug before she leaves and Larry, who is unaware of her coming to the house for dinner and bonding with the family, is speechless.

As I start to share with Larry all that happened at Kate's apartment, my phone vibrates. It shows an incoming call from an unknown caller. I'm hesitant to answer, but I've got a policeman outside the house and a behemoth inside, so I take the call. It's Gwen's mom, Anne, on the other end.

I had met Gwen's folks about five months ago when they were in Cleveland for a visit to watch one of her fencing or debate matches at school. I had volunteered to give them the nickel tour of the *Chronicle*, and the four of us had gone out for dinner before they took in a show at Playhouse Square, which I had Gwen review in my stead to impress her parents.

Anne and I make small talk for a minute, and then she tells me that she's worried about her daughter. She hasn't heard from Gwen in days and called her apartment and the newspaper but could not reach her. The receptionist at the *Chronicle* gave her my number. "I hope you don't mind," she says.

I tap the speakerphone option so that Larry, who now has a vested interest in Gwen, can hear the conversation.

I am about to explain that I had tried to contact Gwen myself after the opening night debacle at *Sweeney Todd*, but Larry vigorously waves me off, since it is clear that Anne doesn't know about what had transpired or how Gwen had been so dramatically affected. I tell her that Gwen is probably just overwhelmed with schoolwork and will no doubt surface when things ease up.

"Why, Gwen's been expelled from school," she says as if I were already in on that intel, "so that can't be the reason. Honestly, I was so very grateful that the newspaper was OK with her still working there. You must have put in a good word."

I was about to explain that the paper couldn't possibly house an intern who was no longer connected to a school but, again, Larry waves me off since this news would only serve to further upset Gwen's mom.

I want to ask about the circumstances of Gwen's expulsion, but I anticipate Larry's reaction and just say, "How can I help?"

Anne gives me the address to Gwen's small apartment in the Clifton Boulevard neighborhood just west of the city and asks whether I would look in on her. "Not calling me is so unlike her," says Anne on the verge of tears. "She must be so upset. I hope she's taking her medicine. She'd probably prefer to talk to you than her mom right now. You've been a good friend and a great mentor. She really looks up to you."

"I'd be happy to go by her apartment. I'm sure she's fine."

When I hang up, I look at Larry for his take on things. "Well, this isn't good," he utters, proving once again the value of his advanced degree in psychology and years of professional experience. "Gwen's been keeping things from us," says Larry, "and she's been keeping things from her mom. She must be terribly depressed and despondent."

"What medicine?" I ask.

"During opening night, when I was comforting Gwen, she opened her purse backstage to find something to calm her down and I heard so many vials rattling that I thought she was minoring in pharmacology. That's the main reason I tried to call her, to make sure she was taking her prescriptions as prescribed. Ethically, I couldn't share that with you but her mom just did. I think Gwen's in trouble. Witnessing a murder on top of all the other stresses in her life can't be good."

The words "What should we do?" came out of my mouth, but we were both already reaching for our coats and heading out the door to my car. Several minutes later, I return to the house to look for my car keys.

Chapter 32

You Are Loved and You Are Missed

L ARRY AND I agree that I will approach Gwen's apartment alone to see whether she is there and to get myself invited inside. I have a relationship with her that predates Larry and, as her mom had said, she looks up to me. If she is amenable and in need, I will text Larry and have him come in to offer one of his patented bear hugs and a little trauma therapy.

"She might not want to see either of us," he warns, "which is fine. Just do a quick assessment of her mental health. Make sure she is taking care of herself physically, see if she is eating and sleeping, make sure she is not inebriated. Tell her that she is loved and missed, and then walk away."

I park in front of the apartment building on the opposite side of the street and Larry pulls the lever on his passenger seat to lower the back so he can hide from view, which is not only silly but an exercise in futility, given the size of him. I walk to the entryway of the building, ring the buzzer by Gwen's name, and hear her voice asking, "Who's there?"

"Hey Gwen, it's Asher Kaufman. I've been calling and calling to see how you are holding up since *Sweeney Todd*. Can I come in for a minute?" There's a long pause, and then the door buzzes open and in I go, keeping the entrance open with a stone so that Larry can have easy access if need be.

Her efficiency apartment is in the rear on the first floor. When I knock on the door, Gwen opens it without saying a word. As I enter, I am immediately accosted by Gwen's huge golden retriever, who gives me a few slobbering licks before offering me her butt for obligatory scratching. "That's Chloe," she says.

From the entranceway, I notice that Gwen's place is clean (on the drive over, Larry said that cleaning reflects a person's healthy control over their environment) and that none of the mirrors have been smashed (Larry said that breakage of furniture would be an indication of manic rage). I also notice that nothing in the apartment had been painted black (Larry didn't mention this in the car, but painting everything black is always a sign of trouble in the psychological thrillers I watch on TV).

Everything looks fine, except for the clutter. The limited living space between the tiny kitchenette and the futon that serves as Gwen's bed/office is littered with dog toys, schoolbooks, and her fencing gear, including a black gym bag filled with an underarm and chest protector, a white jacket, mask, and gloves. A freestanding human form training dummy used for target practice—called BOB, short for Body Opponent Bag—and a rack with assorted épées take up an entire corner of the place. Another corner is dominated by Chloe's beanbag bed. Shelves on the walls bear the weight of many high school and college awards for speech and debate, as well as numerous trophies for fencing.

"How are you doing?" I ask. "Are you eating? Sleeping? You're not drinking, are you? You are loved and you are missed." I suck at this.

"Did you swallow a wellness manual?"

"Pretty much," I admit, and try to laugh it off before getting back to business. "Opening night was a nightmare. I was so worried about you. So was Mark. Larry, my friend who's the really big therapist you met that night, is concerned as well."

"Yeah, it was a really tough night."

I start engaging Gwen in small talk just to relieve the awkwardness of me being here and to make her comfortable confiding in me. I tell her about the crazy conversation the cast had about the old melodrama *The Drunkard* at the Towson Moose Lodge in Baltimore while we were waiting in the theater to talk to Detective Brandstätter, but she reminds me that she was there when that happened. "I was traumatized," she says. "I didn't lose my hearing."

Larry might interpret Gwen's snarkiness as a sign of mental health, but I'm not a fan. This is as good a time as any to mention that I spoke to her mom.

"Did she tell you that I was expelled from school?" Gwen asks after I tell her about the phone call. She can see from the concern on my face that her mom had.

"I was accused of plagiarism. I got some 'B' grades on theater reviews I had written for my arts journalism assignments. I never get low grades like that. Anyway, I tried writing the next few reviews in your style, since you've been so successful, but then I got one 'B-' after another. I figured I just wasn't capturing your style, so I submitted some of your reviews with my name on them just to see whether it was me or you that was the problem. My professor found the writing—your writing—to be pedestrian and pedantic.

"I get that a lot."

"When I confronted the professor and told him those reviews had been written by a professional, I was charged with academic misconduct and got suspended for plagiarism. I went home for a week to feel sorry for myself, and then I came back to my apartment to get on with my life, such that it is."

"Well, your professor is an idiot. You were just challenging his competence by submitting my reviews with your name on them. You weren't really trying to capitalize on my work, you were trying to figure out how to improve your own."

I told her that I would be happy to write to her school to get her reinstated. And I told her to call her mom. "You are loved and you are missed."

As I get up to leave, Chloe comes over for one last butt scratch.

When I get out into the apartment building's hallway, I congratulate myself on administering some prime mentoring and quality mental health care. Larry would have been proud. Our work here is done.

Chapter 33

Touché

As I HEAD to the car, I give Gwen's mom a call to report that her daughter is fine. I tell her that Gwen's expulsion was the result of a bad decision on her part and a professor's overreaction to it. "I think I can help in getting the charge of plagiarism dropped."

There's a long pause, which I interpret as Anne's inability to find the words to thank me, until she asks if Gwen told me the rest of the reason for getting kicked out of her school.

"She was also reviewing plays for the campus newspaper and turning in your old reviews of them with her name," says an emotionally exhausted Anne. "When they emptied the locker she has at the school paper, they found clippings of your reviews with your headshot cut out and your name scratched off. There were piles of them. This is so disturbing. That's why Gwen was expelled by the school, and why her doctor put her on new medication."

My next call is to Mark at the *Chronicle* to see whether he is aware of Gwen's expulsion. He is not. "She would have been immediately released by the paper," he tells me, adding that "Gwen was let go from the paper over a week ago for a different reason. She was assigned to review a few shows while you were in Taos, and her writing got progressively odd. There was less about what was happening on stage and more about what was going on backstage with the production crew. I reminded her that this is not what our readers want, but she ignored me and became belligerent."

"Yeah. I've seen that side of her first-hand."

"When things didn't improve, I fired her and had to send some new intern from sports to review *Sweeney Todd*. When he got home from the show, covered in blood, he texted his resignation and said he was changing his major to something that didn't require ever leaving his house."

"The day after the murder you called to ask me if I was OK, and you also asked about Gwen. I had assumed you were worried about her because she was at the show to review it."

"No. I knew the two of you were pretty close, and I just wanted to find out how she was doing after getting canned. Why was she at the show?"

Before I turn around to return to Gwen's apartment with a new set of concerns about her well-being, I speed dial Larry but get sent right to his voicemail. "In need of your services," is the message I leave.

Gwen's door is unlocked. I knock, walk in and yell "hello?" Chloe jumps up from her bed and comes running to greet me with her tail wagging and tongue flapping. Gwen gets up from her futon with less enthusiasm.

"You didn't tell me the whole truth about your expulsion. And you never mentioned getting fired at the *Chronicle*."

A blank-faced Gwen takes a huge, exacerbated breath as she surrenders to the fact that some explanation for her actions is now warranted.

"After I reviewed your production of *As You Like It* Kate sent a long email to the paper stating how disappointed she was that yet another critic for the *Chronicle* hadn't even mentioned stage management. I didn't even know that was a thing."

"It isn't. But it seems to be a bone of contention for her."

"I felt terrible that someone at North Coast Theater was disappointed in me, since I'm just starting out as a critic, so I called the theater and asked whoever answered to have Kate give me a call. She did, and we talked for a long time. She told me that stage management is essential but underappreciated and underreported. She seemed fragile and desperate for recognition, so I promised her that I would try to work stage management into every review I wrote."

"You agreed with her?"

"Of course not. It was an empty promise. But when I got expelled for plagiarism, I knew it was just a matter of time before I got fired from the *Chronicle* and I wanted Kate to owe me and be an ally. She loved seeing stage management featured in my reviews, and I told Kate that the only way I could continue to do this in the future was to become the permanent critic for the *Chronicle*. And the only way that would happen is if you and your pedestrian writing disappeared."

With that, Gwen takes a step over to the rack of épées, grabs one, and walks back to me with the business end of the weapon pointing in my direction. "Time to finish what I started."

I instinctively let out a laugh at the absurdity of this moment and open my mouth to say something remarkably witty to mask my alarm. But, as I do, she lunges, and the sword strikes me square in the chest.

"Ow! Damn it, Gwen!" I shout, but there's no blood and I'm not dead. Not even close.

Gwen stands upright, takes aim, and lunges again at exactly the same location with exactly the same outcome. She pulls back the sword and sees that this is one of the training weapons she uses when dueling with others on her team, which has a dull metal nub snapped over the sharp tip she uses for target practice on the pock-marked BOB. She whacks the tip of the blade hard on the floor with impressive flourish and the nub goes flying, which sets Chloe to barking, eager to fetch.

"Hold it!" I holler, in part to stall in case the psychology cavalry is about to come to the rescue, and in part to figure out what the hell is going on. "You wanted me dead? That's what opening night was all about?"

"Yup."

"You gave Kate the razor?"

"I did."

"That's insane! And why kill me in Cleveland and not in Taos? I could be just as dead in New Mexico."

"I wanted to be there to watch."

"So you didn't want Andrew Ganz killed?"

"I was as weirded out as everyone when he nearly landed in my lap. That was all Kate. She must have really hated him."

Gwen is done talking, and as she positions herself for a lethal lunge, Larry bursts through the door, which intensifies Chloe's barking jag and tail wagging. Seeing what's transpiring, Larry allows his forward momentum to clumsily knock me out of the way just as Gwen's sword stabs him in the stomach.

"Ow! Damn it, Gwen!" he shouts, but again no blood because Larry's woolly mammoth sweater proves to be as impenetrable as it is ugly. Gwen attempts to pull back the sword for another strike, but the weapon is tangled in matted knots, thick hair and mega knitting—like a finger stuck in one of those toy Chinese handcuff traps—and is not going anywhere.

I use this opportunity to right myself and dive at Gwen, driving my shoulder hard into her chest, and plowing her into the ground as I had done so effectively to Sweeney Todd. As Goldberg had done to the Undertaker, Diamond Dallas Page, and Lord Steven Regal. And as Nancy Drew had done, metaphorically, to Dwayne Powers in the novel *Stay Tuned For Danger*, which is one of Zoey's favorites. My wife's, too.

There is a lot going on inside my head, all of it random, irrational, and fleeting, as I lie on top of Gwen and as a triumphant Chloe comes over with the nub in her mouth. I marvel at how well Gwen took the hit and figure that fencing must be very aerobic. I'm momentarily amused at the sight of a sword sticking straight out of Larry's belly without Gwen attached to it. And I swear that I will never do a Plimpton ever again.

A little late to the game, the plainclothes cop who was assigned to my house and followed my car to Gwen's apartment enters the door to see where we went and what the shouting was all about. Chloe runs over to give him some love. The officer helps remove the sword from Larry and, as I dismount Gwen, he takes her into custody.

"What took you so long?" I ask Larry, as we watch Gwen cuffed and removed.

"I'm on call. I was on the phone consulting with a patient," says Larry as he pokes at the hole that now exists in the front of his sweater. "Boy, you sure did a lousy job assessing Gwen's state of mind."

"But I got a confession," I reply. "Who's the priest now?"

Chapter 34

Nicknames

THE DAY AFTER Gwen's arrest, Larry and I meet at the downtown precinct to give a report about what had happened at her apartment. We are escorted to Detective Brandstätter's glass-enclosed office, asked to wait, and take our uncomfortable standard-issue seats.

A few minutes later, the detective enters the office, tosses some manila file folders on the desk, and takes her seat. She is not happy with us. I pick up a file labeled "forensics" and find Gwen's spiral notebook from the night of the murder, which has been largely freed of the hemoglobin coating. "Don't bother opening the notebook," says the detective. "It's got no writing in it. Gwen wasn't at the theater to take notes."

Larry picks up a file that contains a copy of Gwen's academic records reporting her expulsion and including her plagiarized essays. I can see that "Pedestrian" is written in bold red letters by her professor and circled at the top of one of them, along with the grade "C." I suppose it was an act of kindness by Gwen to tell me that the essay had earned a "B-" before she tried to skewer me with her sword. But for someone as tightly wound and competitive as her, I can see how a "C" would set her off on a destructive path.

I'm about to pick up the third file, but the detective informs me that it contains a handwriting match between the signature on Gwen's internship contract with the *Chronicle* and the false name she had signed when she delivered a package at the theater's stage door on opening night.

"All this is what I would have shared with you," scolds the detective as she leans forward in her chair, "had you let me know your plans to visit Gwen at her apartment. I would have recommended that you not do that."

Larry and I sit in silence, not at all enjoying the spanking we are receiving or that every uniformed passersby can observe it through the glass walls.

"You put yourselves at risk," she adds. "What you did is best left to the professionals."

"I got stabbed," says Larry, hoping that this would make everything all right.

"I got a confession," I say, for the same reason.

Settling back in her chair, Detective Brandstätter tells us that the incarcerated Kate has been talking her fool head off now that she's traded the stark but private and relatively comfortable cage for a cold and crowded concrete cell. And when she was told that Gwen had been caught as well, Kate realized that there was no reason to keep secrets about what had transpired. She wanted to put things in order because, well, that's what stage managers do.

Kate had been bent toward despair and had had thoughts of revenge for quite a while, but she admitted that she had lacked the initiative and the imagination to forge any kind of plan and put it into practice. It wasn't until Gwen's attention, promise of notoriety, and go-getter attitude had entered the picture that things got real.

During the Cleveland run of *As You Like It*, the two had frequently met, commiserated, and bonded. When the cast and crew moved to Taos to rehearse and perform *Sweeney Todd,* the two had planned and plotted by phone. They agreed on where in the musical my murder should occur, and both agreed that opening night in Cleveland would draw the greatest attention to my demise. This, in turn, would facilitate Gwen's stepping in as my immediate replacement. Gwen had even typed out on her computer at home a rough-draft first paragraph review of the ill-fated show before leaving for the theater, should the *Chronicle* need coverage. Its title: "All of Us Deserve to Die."

Both Gwen and Kate had taken solace in the fact that while they carefully planned my murder, neither would actually commit it. Of course, Kate would be a bit more hands-on with her own plan to kill Andrew Ganz—the drugging and the dragging—but, again, the actual killing would be done by someone else.

During the preview performance prior to opening night, Kate had rehearsed going up to the barbershop before curtain to simulate replacing one razor for another to make sure she did not call attention to herself. Even if she did, a stage manager doing a final walk-through of the set is a familiar sight. The preview performance had also afforded the opportunity to rehearse leaving the cage and walking down the aisle while calling light cues with a wireless headset and making her way backstage toward the temporary changing booths. The dark house and her black clothing made her virtually invisible. It all went smoothly.

The two agreed that on opening night, Gwen would get to the theater's box office early to pick up the press ticket designated for the *Chronicle's* critic before whomever the paper sent as her replacement was able to claim it. And she would stand in the lobby reviewing a playbill while actually watching for anyone in attendance who might be from the *Chronicle* and know that she was no longer a working critic. If all was clear and the plan was a go, she would run back to her car before the lobby lights flashed to signal fifteen minutes before curtain, grab the package containing the razor and gloves, and deliver it to the stage door before heading to her seat in the theater. If things were problematic, Gwen would head back to her car, get in, and go home.

"It was a clever plan," admits the detective, "and I'm glad you're not dead, Asher. But I'm angry that you and Larry put yourselves in harm's way."

"Yeah, we hadn't given much thought to the 'harm's way' scenario," I admit. Larry nods in the affirmative.

The detective looks at me a moment, shaking her head in disbelief at our recklessness, and then announces that the fellows on the force have come up with my nickname. "Asher, we are calling you 'The Metsh.'"

"The what?"

"It's Yiddish," explains Detective Brandstätter. "You should know this. It means a good person who talks and talks, and argues, and talks."

"You mean 'mensch'."

"Not my idea."

Larry and I look at each other and smile at Detective Brandstätter's failed attempt at Yiddish. We are admittedly touched by it as well.

Metsh, it is.

Chapter 35

Quite Enough of Sondheim

FROM THE EDITOR: This is the final behind-the-scenes article by theater critic Asher Kaufman about his adventures in North Coast Theater's production of *Sweeney Todd,* which is now on stage in Cleveland.

For the past week, this newspaper, among many others, has been filled with stories about the tragedy that took place during last week's opening night production of *Sweeney Todd.* After no shortage of mourning, healing, and restructuring, the company's powers-that-be decided to move forward with the Cleveland run of the musical. With Gwen, our arts journalism intern, indisposed for the foreseeable future, I stepped away from the production as an actor and moved back into my role as the critic for the *Chronicle.*

My remarkably subjective review of opening night 2.0 appears elsewhere in this issue of the paper. The show is certainly more impressive when viewed from the audience side of the proscenium arch, though it is so much more intriguing—and apparently dangerous—when experienced from the inside.

It was humbling to see how easily my character was assumed by another ensemble member. And while watching the show, I felt a twinge of melancholy when the actor now playing my part walked off stage in the drunken arms of the actor now playing Freddie Muñoz's part during "God, That's Good!" But when Sweeney sang "Jo-han-na" and the trap door opened, I was happy to be in my cushy seat in the sixth row of the house rather than in the reclining chair in the barbershop at center stage. I mean, *real* happy.

I was told that, at 7:25 p.m., just before the performance began, the cast of fourteen formed a circle on the stage behind the closed curtain, held hands, and—as has been our custom—offered up some positive thoughts for our ailing colleague Charlie. There was a moment of silence for Freddie and Andrew as well. And, just before taking their places, everyone said, "What the f---?!" for me. A new backstage theater tradition has been born, to go with "break a leg" and "see you on the ice."

Opening night 2.0 was sold out, and the show received two loud, prolonged standing ovations. The first occurred when the curtain rose at the start of the show to acknowledge the cast's resolve and applaud North Coast Theater's perseverance. I stood as well. The second was for a performance very well done.

Neither Larry, Patty, nor Detective Brandstätter were in attendance. They had had quite enough of Sondheim.

In his *The New Yorker* review of a Broadway revival of *Sweeney Todd* not long ago, theater critic John Lahr noted that the musical is "deeply and hopelessly savage" and "depicts a society that feels itself irredeemably lost." It has also been written that, in *Sweeney Todd*, Sondheim and Wheeler have succeeded in writing a morality tale for a brutish world that doubts the very existence of morality.

It is hard to argue with that. The 19th century London

society depicted in this musical is practically impervious to goodness, what with Judge Turpin's false imprisonment of the young Sweeney Todd, the villainous acts of Mrs. Lovett, the antics of impostor and blackmailer Adolfo Pirelli, the crooked Beadle Bamford, the corrupt asylum keeper Jonas Fogg, and so on.

But it is important to look past the savagery in this musical to find the moral of and the morality in the story: that every evildoer gets their comeuppance. Even Sweeney Todd realizes, and accepts, that his vengeance comes at a great personal cost. And in the real world, in the aftermath of our opening night, so, too, do Kate and Gwen.

A single sheet of paper has been inserted into tonight's playbill announcing the casting changes and noting that the assistant stage manager, Jasmine, has been promoted. Let's hope, for everyone's sake, that she takes to a life in the cage better than her predecessor. As you'll see in my review, I make it a point to mention the stage management. Just a little and just to be safe.

Epilogue

THE PHONE RINGS and a receptionist answers.

"Hello, Metsh, Priest, and Brandstätter Detective Agency."

"Yeah, hi. My theater company is in terrible trouble, and I think I'm in danger. We will be performing Ken Ludwig's *A Comedy of Tenors*. Does Asher Kaufman do farce?"

Acknowledgments

This novella is dedicated to Judy, for her loving support, gentle tweaking, and slaps to the side of my head during our long walks down short paths.

Special thanks to Vicky Bussert, Tom Ford, Corrie Purdum, and Lauren Calevich. Without their insight into the innerworkings of a *Sweeney Todd* production, this murder would not have been possible.

Here's an 11th hour thank you to those who I entrusted with earlier drafts of this work and whose feedback made it between the covers: AJ Abelman, Zach Bartz, Rich Leder, Larry Moss, Gwendolyn Kochur, Fred Sternfeld, Randi Sternfeld, Nancy Minter, Mark Goren, and Jo Goren.

Thanks to *Cleveland Jewish News* publisher Kevin S. Adelstein, who granted permission to use excerpts from my published work that appear here under Asher Kaufman's byline.

In Chapter 5, the tale of Edith Webster was informed by United Press International, "Playing Death Scene, Actress Suffers Fatal Heart Attack," *Los Angeles Times*, Nov. 24, 1986.

In Chapter 13, quotes from the following actual theater reviews were applied to fictious performers and performances: Ben Brantley's "Where an Angel Fearlessly Treads," *The New York Times*, Oct. 21, 2005; David Cote's "Scandalous," *Time Out New York*, Nov. 15, 2012; Terry Teachout's "Wheel This Barrow Out of Town," *The Washington Post*, Dec. 2, 2011.

In Chapter 35, quotes from critic John Lahr's *New Yorker* review of *Sweeney Todd* were extracted from Leah Libresco's "If Only Angels Would Prevail: The Moral Tragedy of Sweeney Todd," *Ethika Politika*, March 3, 2014.

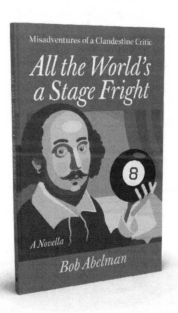

All the World's a Stage Fright
Misadventures of a Clandestine Critic
Bob Abelman

A drama critic takes an acting role with a top-tier
theater company in a stunt to boost readership and
gets more of a story than he bargained for. Despite
a debilitating Shakespeare phobia, he must share
the stage with actors he's panned in the past and
avoid getting panned himself by fellow critics. Vivid,
realistic, behind-the-curtain action.

More information at **www.grayco.com**